Bushwhacker

When young Hal Coburn came back from the long and savage Civil War, he hoped for a return to his former peaceful life. Instead he found a deadly homecoming of hostility and subdued anger, and the dark cloud of a memory that still haunted the minds of all who looked at him. Justice and revenge are often hard to separate and where there is no help from the law only the gun can even the score. The price for Hal was high. All his future life lay scattered before him in blood and gold across a trail that led only into the dark.

Bushwhacking seems a low way of searching for justice but sometimes it looks like the only way of bringing some right where there was none before. The result can be as savage as war itself as Hal was soon destined to discover.

Bushwhacker

BILL MORRISON

A Black Horse Western

ROBERT HALE · LONDON

© Bill Morrison 2004
First published in Great Britain 2004

ISBN 0 7090 7572 3

Robert Hale Limited
Clerkenwell House
Clerkenwell Green
London EC1R 0HT

Typeset by
Derek Doyle & Associates, Liverpool.
Printed and bound in Great Britain by
Antony Rowe Limited, Wiltshire

1

Well, it was all over and he should try to forget it. He was glad to see the end of the war with all its horror and pain and grief but months had passed since the news that it was over had come through and still it was with him, bringing back the terrible scenes he and thousands of others had witnessed. It was still too fresh in his mind but he hoped its memories would fade and he could open his life again on the page where he had left it four years before.

He smiled faintly, his thin young features creasing around the mouth. He raised his head and narrowed his dark eyes against the wind, which blew wisps of black hair across his brow. All around, the undulating grasslands seemed to drift like the waves of the sea towards the low hills on the horizon. Ahead he could see a glint of water in the afternoon sunlight. He recognized it as a stream he had known in boyhood and his heart lifted as he saw another sign that he was nearing home. He drew his horse to a gentle halt and twisted in the saddle.

'That's Briarbush over yonder,' he said cheerfully. 'Not much of a river but it's sure good to see! Not so far to go now, Blick!'

His companion on the mare behind him grinned in response, pleasant black face splitting into the flashing grin. He was a smiler, was Blick, and it took a heap of trouble to wipe that easy, unworried expression away even for a few minutes.

'Sure, Mr Coburn, fine thing after all this time, I guess!'

'Hal.'

'Yeah, Mr Hal.'

The 'mister' was unnecessary, as Hal had pointed out a dozen times before, but it was a difficult habit to break. Blick still tended to see his relationship with whites in the only way he had known throughout his life. Hal had met him a couple of years back in a camp near Springhorn Flats, where he had limped around with a bullet wound in his leg but was still able to attend to the horses. Before that, Blick had been in a black infantry regiment fighting against the Confederacy but had been shot down in a skirmish. His comrades had survived that fight but had gone on to be wiped out the next week in a fierce battle which had left

6

none of them alive. The Rebs were not looking to take any prisoners that day so Blick had been fortunate not to have been there, but he had never said so.

The wound in his leg had healed and, at the same time, Hal had struck up a friendship with him. A mutual respect had developed which had quickly transcended the common barriers which were everywhere to be found. Hal liked the black soldier's honesty and good humour and his lack of bitterness for the events of the past. When he learned that Blick had nowhere to go after the war, he had suggested he come back to the family farm, way up north, where he could at least earn a living and have a home and maybe even some kind of a future, though it was hard to imagine what that might be.

The thought of arriving home at last made Hal's heart thump. Many a time he had dreamed of it when he had been sleeping under the stars or was bivouacked out in the rain. He had not heard from his parents for a long time but letters had been few and far between, even when he had been stationed in a regular camp, and recent months had seen his cavalry troop ranging far and wide.

It would be swell to see his parents again. He sighed at the thought and then put heels to his horse as he approached the river.

They dismounted and drank the cool water,

then led their horses down the low bank. Blick was riding a little grey mare that Hal had bought back at the depot at the same time as he had traded his uniform for civilian clothes. He had told himself that the mare would be useful on the farm but he knew his real reason had been to find a way of bringing Blick back with him. As for the uniform, he had been intent upon getting rid of that as quickly as he could. His need to enter again into his old life had seemed to make the change necessary The only thing he had kept was the regimental badge he now carried in the capacious pocket of his jacket. Too many good men had died wearing that badge to leave it behind as if it meant nothing.

Another day must pass before he would come in sight of home The house and land where he had been raised was humble enough, and there had been many a time in the past when he had wearied of it and longed to ride out to a wider world. Maybe that feeling would return sometime but right now he wanted nothing more than to get back to its familiar surroundings, to drink in the welcome and comfort that was always there and to let the war slip away once and for all.

'May as well sleep here tonight, Blick,' he suggested. 'We've ridden far enough today. Horses are needing to rest.'

'Sure thing, Mr Hal,'

As usual, Blick took the suggestion as an order. Hal sighed as he drew the saddle to the ground and ground-tethered his mount, making certain that it could graze over a sufficient area. The corn they had carried with them was finished but it did not matter for very soon the animals would be in his home paddock.

Blick did the same for the mare and then went down to the stream to fill a mess-tin with clear water. As he bent over, the wind caught his checked shirt and for a second his back was exposed, showing the old scars of a whipping. Hal knew he had been a slave before running off in his youth. Later the war had started and he had joined his regiment. Had it been for some idea of revenge? Could be. It was not always too easy to tell with Blick. That grin seemed to cover his feelings like a blanket.

Late next afternoon they crossed a ridge and saw the farm in the distance. Hal came to a sudden halt and drew in his breath with pleasure. He could make out the roof and chimney and the two elm-trees that had always been there in the background. He sat still in the saddle, eyes full of wonder and delight. Blick was alongside, grinning as if he understood.

'There ain't no place like home, Mr Hal. So they say.'

'They say right.'

But there was no smoke. Always in the past that old chimney had been smoking, sometimes heavy in the winter, but even in the summer there was at least a little smoke, for there was always cooking to attend to or water to boil for washing clothes or removing the farm dirt from weary bodies. Now there was no trace. Hal's sharp eyes could see nothing but a solitary pigeon fluttering about the roof.

Something deflated in his heart. It was if a voice was calling to him over the intervening space, warning him that all was not well.

He spurred his horse forward and Blick followed, smile fading as he caught the feeling of anxiety.

When they reached the gate, they came to a stop, partly because the horses were blown by the sudden gallop, but mainly because the gate was tied shut with a length of old rope. There were weeds everwhere. The shutters were over the windows. There was no sign of life except for the pigeon. No horses, cows, chickens, just nothing.

'Seems like as if . . .' Blick's voice trailed off.

Hal said nothing. He stared at the old stone-and-timber building created by the hard labour of his grandfather so many years before. Always it had seemed welcoming even in the worst days, when things were going badly and it was hard to make a living from this small stretch of land. Now it was as if it just stared back at him, as a stranger might have done, with no trace of recognition.

He dismounted, untied the rope from the gate and walked up the narrow path to the front door. Blick remained behind as if there was need to attend the horses but with his face set in sudden dismay and with some feeling that he should keep his distance. The door opened with a creak of the latch and Hal entered the living-room from which he had marched away with mixed feelings so long before.

It looked about the same. The old deal table was set in the middle with four chairs tucked half-under it. The sideboard still held the glass vase in which prairie flowers had often bloomed. The faded picture of his grandparents was still on the wall above the fireplace, now cold and empty.

He went through the other two rooms, each containing a bed, neatly made up with blankets that he remembered well. Then he went out of the back door and looked across the vegetable patch, which was now a riot of weeds. The old familiar rain-barrel still stood by the wall and a rusting fork leaned against the fence.

He had a terrible feeling of foreboding. A memory flashed into his mind of a deserted house he and other troopers had entered away down south on the Texan border. It had been empty too except for the corpses of two men hanging above the porch and the body of a woman in the front room. That had been the work of deserters from one side or the other, men who had turned into bandits, the kind of diseased human beings that war always turned up out of the dirt.

But there was no sign of violence here and no trace of robbery or destruction. It was as if the inhabitants had just walked out and left everything behind. There was no way, however, that they would have done so. He knew the answer almost before he had framed the question in his mind. . . . His parents were dead. That was why there had been no letter and no message.

Still, there ought to have been a message – if not directly to him then through the army high command so that he could be informed wherever he had been serving at the time. If his folks had died of disease or in some strange accident, one of the neighbours, or one of the leading citizens of Sandstone Creek, ought to have sent word.

He did not move for some time. The realization that something terrible had happened to his parents sank in only slowly. At last he turned and walked back to the living-room where he stood a little longer before he pulled open the wooden door and went back down the path to where Blick still held the horses.

'They ain't here, Blick,' he grunted, his voice unexpectedly hoarse. 'It looks like . . .' He nodded and looked up at the sky without finishing the sentence. 'We need to ask around.'

There was another homestead a couple of miles further on in the general direction of Sandstone. Before they reached it, they saw the bent figure of a man carrying wood towards a mule-cart. He wore a black hat pulled well down over his head and his clothes were dirty and torn. He squinted up at them from behind a long nose, his face showing astonishment. Hal remembered him very well as the owner of the place – a widower who had lived on his own for a long time.

'Hey, Fergus,' said Hal, trying to keep his voice even. 'You remember me? Hal Coburn. I just got back.'

Fergus stared up at him, uncertainty and confusion evident in his eyes.

'Yeah, sure, Hal, o'course . . . Good to see you. . . .'

'As I say, Fergus, I just got back. This here's Blick. Good friend of mine.'

The little eyes showed surprise but there came no further greeting.

'Fergus.' Hal's tone held a hint of irritation. He was finding difficulty in keeping a grip of his feelings. 'My place is empty. Folks have vanished. I never knew anything about it. What happened?'

'Well, thing is . . . I don't rightly know. Well, I guess . . .'

'What happened to my mother, Fergus?'

'She died. Sorry about thet, Hal They jest found her dead. Still lying in bed, I heard tell. Thet feller who helped with your stock – he found her when he went up and couldn't get no answer at the door. She was jest dead.'

'How come?'

'Don't know. Nobody knew. Thet was the way it was. Sorry, Hal. . . .'

'My father? What about him?'

Fergus turned away and fumbled with the pile of timber on the cart.

'Don't know about Billy. Sorry, I can't say nothin' about thet! I never saw nothin'. Didn't have no part in it.'

'What the hell you talking about, Fergus?'

'You need to ask somebody else about it, Hal. I ain't never been mixed up in it at all. No sirree! Sorry, Hal. Ain't much of a homecoming, but it's nothin' to do with me!'

He climbed up on to the cart and cracked the reins so that the mule was set in motion. Catching up with him to carry on the questioning would have been easy but Hal suddenly felt there was no point. Fergus had nothing more to say . . .

They did not move for some minutes as the mule-cart gradually disappeared round a bend. Hal felt as if his mind had turned to stone. He could not think clearly. Blick sat in the saddle in silence, glancing at his companion's back and then across the landscape of open grassland, punctuated here and there by cultivated fields. He sensed Hal's trouble but knew there was nothing he could say that might help.

'We'll ride into Sandstone,' decided Hal, at last. 'Maybe we can learn something there.'

Sandstone Creek was a small town a few miles further on. They took an easy pace, knowing the horses to be tiring. On the way, they rode along the banks of the river. This too was the Briarbush, grown broader now and flowing swiftly. On the further bank the ground rose to woodland. Even at a distance, Hal could see men working there, felling and hauling timber. Beyond that, in an area of cleared land there was a fine house, the biggest in the region, built mostly of stone but with an upper storey of wood. Hal knew it belonged to Pete Clement, the richest rancher and landowner for many miles around. Somehow, the house seemed even bigger now, after four years.

Hal turned his eyes from it, too full of his own worries to think much about anything else. He scarcely looked up until they reached the outskirts of the little town and began to ride down towards the main street. People glanced at him as he passed and then turned quickly away. He knew most of these folks from the past but they seemed not to recognize him. Men on the sidewalk looked suddenly in the other direction. A lady jumped as if startled and then hurried into the general store.

Hal rode on in silence, making up his mind to look in at the sheriff's office, but before he got there he stopped at the gate of the churchyard, another disturbing thought shooting into his brain. He jumped to the ground, pushed open the little wicker gate and strode up the narrow path amongst the tombstones. Almost all were old but not far from the main door of the church there stood a stone with fresh lettering bearing his mother's name – Mary Coburn. The sight of it shocked him and he could not move for some minutes. He had guessed she was dead from the moment of his arrival at the house but this confirmation seemed to stab him to the heart. At length, he pulled himself together and took off his hat in a gesture of respect. Just then he realized that his father's name was not on the stone and anger came into his mind, pushing out grief for the time being.

He turned abruptly and made his way back towards the gate. On the way he caught sight of another new stone and walked over the grass to read the inscription. It was the grave of Becky Hunter. His face registered surprise. He remembered Becky as a young girl of about nine years old, quite pretty, very lively, but reputed to be of less than average intelligence. The less kindly of her neighbours were inclined to refer to her as being 'a bit touched' or 'half crazy'. Certainly, Hal remembered her as being wild and unpredictable in her behaviour and not too bright in her mind. He pursed his lips now at the thought of such a young person dying. It could have been anything, he guessed, fever or some disease. Plenty of children died. It was always sad.

But his own troubles were uppermost in his mind. His mother was dead of some mysterious illness. He knew within himself that his father was also dead but, in his case, there was no grave. That seemed to mean there was no body.

Hal stood at the gate for a moment, staring back at his mother's headstone and then turned and walked swiftly along the street. Blick followed, also on foot, and leading the two horses.

When Hal reached the sheriff's office, he did not hesitate before bounding up the few wooden stairs and pushing open the door. The sheriff, Somerville, sat there engrossed in a ledger but looked up at the sudden interruption. His lank grey hair hung over his ears. For a moment the grey moustache over his upper lip trembled as he opened his mouth in surprise.

They stared at one another in mutual recognition. Somerville had been sheriff as long as Hal could remember. He was a man who was known to prefer a quiet life but that was not so hard to find in Sandstone where nothing much seemed to

happen and the only trouble might be the occa-
sional drunk in Murphy's saloon. Hal had never
quite known what to think of Somerville. It did not
seem to him that the sheriff had ever been put to
the test.

Somerville looked sharply at Hal. For the past
year he had known, at the back of his mind, that
this meeting would come about. Often he had
found himself hoping that it never would but that
would have meant Hal not coming back from the
war and the sheriff did not like to believe he could
ever harbour such thoughts.

His mouth tightened under his moustache as he
looked at the young man. Hal seemed older and
tougher by a good many years than he had on his
departure. He had the lean, hard look which many
soldiers brought back with them. There was black
stubble on his chin and a tiny white scar on his
right cheek. He was wearing a deerskin jacket
under which a service revolver bulged. The most
prominent thing about him right now, though,
were his eyes, which were full of anxiety and
scarcely controlled agitation.

For a moment neither spoke, then Somerville
broke the silence, keeping his voice as calm as he
was able.

'Hey, good to see you, Hal! Glad you're back
safe and sound from thet goddamned war! When
did you . . . ?'

'I've been home.' Hal felt like shouting out loud but fought against the impulse. 'I've seen my mother's grave. What the blazes . . . ?'

'It was too bad, Hal, but she just died. Nobody knew jest why.'

'What about my father? What happened to him? He ain't around the farm. He would never be away anywheres. He's dead too – thet right?'

Somerville hesitated. This was going to be as bad as he had ever expected. Why the hell did he have to be the one person in this damned town to face down young Hal Coburn at a time like this? He knew the reason. Nobody else would want to say. He didn't want to either but he was the one official around to whom the young feller would come to hear the truth. The other one, of course, was the minister, the Reverend Cranberry, but he was never to be seen except on Sundays. The rest of the week he spent over at Magpie Drop with his lady friend.

'Listen, Hal, there ain't no use getting too het up about this.'

'Het up?'

'Well, of course, your father being dead ain't no laughing matter – I mean – but thing is there's nothing we can do about it, so keep calm. All right?'

'I'm listening, for God's sake!'

'Your pa, Billy, he got killed . . .'

'Killed?'

'Yeah. There was trouble – a big heap of trouble and he ended up dead.'

Hal said nothing. Something seemed to have clenched his teeth together.

'A lot of folks killed him. They got real riled up. It all got out of hand. I wasn't there otherwise it might have been different. They was like a mob. Mad – like a mob. You see he murdered somebody. It was a girl – young girl by the name of Becky Hunter.'

2

Hal sat down on the chair opposite the sheriff. His legs suddenly felt weak. He had had a thousand shocks over the last few years but this seemed the worst. His mind could not take it in. For a moment, Somerville fell silent. He was relieved that Hal had not turned violent at what had just been said but maybe there was more to come.

'Thing is, Hal,' he went on, 'it was a terrible blow fer everybody. You see, Becky ran off into the country and got herself lost. You know what she was like. Do you remember her? She was just a kid, hardly thirteen years old at the time. She got this crazy idea in her head about gold at the end of the rainbow. I'm pretty sure it was thet lunatic Hokay who put it there. He was talking about some such rubbish that very morning. Well, she and her sister were always short of money after their parents died and when she heard about this gold at the end of the rainbow, she jest run out to look fer it and got lost. You see, it had been raining in the night and all morning and then outcomes the rainbow and Becky goes off like a jack-rabbit. It was thet Hokay guy, sure as guns, though he never did admit it. You all right, Hal?'

'I'm still listening. What about my pa?'

'I'm getting to that. Well, when folks realized she had run off, a lot of the men mounted up and went out to look for her, only it was getting late because she wasn't missed at first. It was some kids who told about her rainbow idea and they had seen her running out of town towards where she thought the rainbow was coming down. The kids were laughing, of course. They jest thought it was funny. Anyhow, the search went on fer a long time. Then just when it was getting dark, they found her. She had been strangled.'

Hal straightened up, eyes staring. Somerville looked at him, his own fingers gripping the desk.

'Yeah, well thing is, she was – there's no easy way of saying this, Hal. She was strangled by your pa's belt. Thet's it. Billy's leather belt was round her neck. He was there too. Pete Clement was the first to find them. He was searching near there at Calfskin Rock. Billy went for a gun and Pete had to shoot him. Then the rest came up. They went out of their minds when they saw Becky and set about kicking and hitting Billy with their rifle butts. You see he was still alive though bleeding like hell from

22

Pete's bullet. Then they all hung him from a tree. I can't say what the hell your pa did thet for. Nothing else had happened to Becky but maybe thet was because Pete got there in t . . .'

For a moment, Somerville hesitated. Hal's hand had strayed to the gun under his jacket.

'Look here, Hal, I'm only telling you what happened. Billy had been acting a bit queer for a while . . .'

'Queer?'

'Well, there was the time he let his cows wander off so thet one of them was killed by wolves. Then, again, he let his tool-shed burn down.'

'Most older guys get absent-minded. What the blazes are you talking about?'

'All right, but this time it was serious. A young girl was murdered. Folks can't forgive a thing like that.'

'Then what?'

'Well, thet was it. Nobody could do any more about it. There was an inquest, of course.'

'But nobody told me! There was no message sent. And what about him? Why ain't he in his grave beside my mother?' Hal looked closely at Somerville, suddenly understanding. 'But you can't bury a murderer on hallowed ground, like in the churchyard – thet it? All right, so where?'

'Nowhere, Hal. Thing is, they left him hanging. Couple of days later Bilt Cameron rode out that way jest to have a look-see but there was nothing. Somebody had cut the rope. Bilt didn't stay long but he couldn't see anything at all.'

Hal knew what was meant. Bilt hadn't seen any chewed remains left by the coyotes.

'How the hell was that?' asked Hal. 'You go out yourself to investigate? No? Ain't it your business to make sure a man gets buried decent?'

'Strictly speaking, no, it ain't, Hal. If he had still been there, I'd have brought him in. That would be evidence but it ain't my job to bury anybody. That's for the relatives.'

'My poor old mother, you mean. And what about this mob? You bring them to trial?'

'Too much of a mix-up. Nobody would have testified against anybody else. Anyhow, Judge Elder sympathized with the folks. He said it was inevitable. As for Pete – he was only defending himself.'

'How come you weren't there when it was all happening? You away chasing rainbows too?'

'Don't get smart, Hal. I know how you feel but going wild won't help. I was searching further out. It was all over by the time I found out about it.'

Hal stood up. Fury and grief and a terrible sense of hopelessness ran through him. He did not look at Somerville again but stalked out through the door, allowing it to slam behind him. Blick was still standing outside. He glanced closely at Hal but did not speak. No word passed between them at all as they rode out of town in the direction of the farm. For a while, Hal felt numb. He could not think. It was only when he saw his parents' roof in the distance that he found his voice enough to tell Blick what had happened. The Negro gasped but could not find any words to say except that he felt real sorry about it.

When they got into the house, dusk had fallen and Blick busied himself lighting the fire with wood from the shed and boiling water for coffee. There was no food except the little they still had with them. Hal sat at the table, almost unaware of Blick's activity. As he sipped his coffee, however, he looked around at the familiar room and began to remember the past, all of which had been sane and honest and worthwhile, and he could not believe that what he had heard could be true.

He made up his mind to find the truth. Tomorrow he would ride out to Calfskin Rock.

In the morning he arose with the sun already up and rode out on his own. He felt he could have no one with him on this day and asked Blick to stick around the farm except for a quick trip into town to buy some food.

It took three hours to reach the vicinity of Calfskin. He remembered the way pretty well through the rugged country but it was difficult going and he reflected with amazement on the wanderings of that poor child, Becky Hunter. She must have become hopelessly lost and have been running, panic-stricken, through this wilderness long after her rainbow had vanished. Then . . . My God! How could it be? What in hell would Billy have been doing out there and how impossible it seemed that he could have done any harm to anyone, far less a little girl!

The rock from which the locality took its name came into sight. Hal stopped and gazed at it from the distance, his heart seeming to stop. . . .

He rode up slowly, fearful of what he might find in spite of the evidence of Bilt Cameron. It took a bit of scouting around to identify the tree that had been used for the hanging. The piece of rope was there, sure enough. It had been cut through and its shortened length moved slowly in the breeze as it had done ever since the terrible day of its use. It had whitened in the sun and had begun to rot. It was too weak now to carry the weight it had taken then. All things rotted. The knowledge had been in his mind since he had listened to Somerville's story, and he shuddered now although the sun was hot upon his back.

What was it he expected to find? Bones? A skull? He had come across such things often enough in the old battlefields of the South and had become hardened to the experience but this was quite different. The image of his father's bones was too horrifying to contemplate. He did not believe he could look upon such a sight and still remain quite sane.

Nevertheless, he rode around slowly, searching the ground unavailingly, then dismounted to resume his search with greater care. There were a few trees in the area and a good deal of scrub scattered throughout the rocks and down the steep little gully not far from the hanging-tree. It was always possible that animals might have carried bones for some distance, so he controlled his nerves and went on diligently looking in all directions.

There was nothing to be found. There were no signs of animals on the ground. It had been a long time, of course, so there could be no tracks now but there might still have been scraps of bone if the body had been just cut down and left. He was not sure how he ought to feel about that but was aware of some sense of relief.

He returned to the tree and stood again, looking at the rope, trying to figure out who had cut it and why. The sheriff had said the mob had been out of its mind with fury which was why the lynching had happened at all. There seemed no doubt that they would have turned to ride back in to town with no thought of taking down the corpse of the man they had just killed. Such an act would have implied regret and no lynching party could afford any such sentiment. A bloody act of vengeance cannot be seen as unjustified by the people who commit it if they are to know any inward peace in the future. Hal had learned that from the war, where there *had* been atrocities but no word of regret uttered to match the uneasiness lurking behind the eyes of those men who had committed them.

He wondered who had been involved in the lynching. Somerville had said nothing about that, with good reason. There was no sense in young Hal Coburn, just back from the war, going around town and searching out his father's killers to question them. That could lead to big trouble.

Somerville had spoken, though, about Pete Clement, who had got to the scene of the murder first and had been forced to shoot in self-defence. Clement was a rich and important man, with ranching and mining interests, who wielded a lot of power in the neighbourhood. Hal remembered seeing Clement's house in the distance as he had ridden into town the day before. It looked as if it was growing bigger, which indicated that the landowner was doing better than ever. In a way it seemed strange that Pete had taken the trouble to join in the search for a half-crazed girl of no importance to him. He was always too busy to bother about matters

that did not seem to impinge upon his own interests.

The more Hal thought about that, the more
unlikely it seemed, but, of course, he might be
quite wrong about Clement. Maybe he had more
heart than he was given credit for, or he might just
have been caught up in the whole event without
really meaning to.

The fact remained, though, that he had shot
Hal's father – or so Somerville had said. There was
no reason to disbelieve the sheriff. The reason had
been self-defence but Hal found that difficult to
visualize. He could not imagine Billy – that easy
going, almost too relaxed old man – pulling a gun
on anybody in almost any circumstance. As far as
Hal could remember, his father had seldom worn
a gun. There had been a couple of times, when
there had been talk of rustlers in the territory,
when he had seen the old man carry that old
Winchester rifle or walk around with a handgun in
his belt, sticking up like a plough-handle from
under his jacket.

But they had never been used and it seemed
unlikely that old Billy had ever been much of a
shot. He had been interested in dairy cattle and
corn seed and not much else. More important,
there had never been a sign of anger or malice in
him.

Well, the sheriff had said he had turned a bit

queer, but hadn't been able to bring up much evidence about that except for what he was supposed to have done with Becky Hunter. Hal closed his eyes for a moment, trying to visualize the scene but it made no sense to him. There were other men who could commit such a terrible crime when in the grip of lust or just plain crazy but somehow Billy Coburn just did not fit.

Nevertheless, he had been out here at the time the girl was killed and Pete Clement had shot him to the ground right on this spot and the crowd had hung him from that tree. It had all happened, sure enough. Hal could not but believe that much of the sheriff's story . . .

He made up his mind to go to the Clement place. He had a right to question Pete about the events of that day. It was Pete who, according to his own evidence, had got into a gunfight with the old man and Hal, just returned from the war, needed to be told, at first hand, exactly how his father had died.

He mounted his patient horse and set off in the direction of the river. An hour passed before the gleam of water came into sight and he turned to rendezvous with it further to the south-east and nearer the ranch.

Eventually the Clement pasture, mostly filled with fine cattle, came into sight. He rode on the trail and saw the house in the near distance against its backdrop of trees. It was an imposing building, by far the finest Hal had ever seen except for the old mansions of the South. The Clements had always had big ideas and had stopped at nothing to achieve them. There had been smaller places all round about in the past but somehow these had been swallowed into the Clement lands.

He saw nobody but a few cattlemen at a distance as he approached, but as he reached a bend in the trail he saw a gate ahead and a group of horsemen close to it. They looked in his direction and he saw one or two of them stiffen in surprise, as if in sudden recognition. The man at the front of the group moved his black horse forward a few paces. Hal knew who he was: Ross Clement, only son of Pete, and heir to all he surveyed.

Hal continued to ride slowly and calmly, keeping his rising feeling of agitation in check. Already, a snake-voice in the back of his head hissed that this meeting was not going to go well. He knew Ross Clement more by reputation than on a personal level. Pete Clement's son was reckoned to be pretty wild and spent more time away from his parents' ranch than working on it. He was fast with a gun – or so they said – and had left a few men dead in Arizona and another one in Mexico. Always in fair fight, gun to gun, eyeball to eyeball. They said that too – after he had told them about it. Nobody in or around Sandstone had seen him draw, except in practice, but he was reckoned to be pretty quick at that and could blast a beer-bottle off the top of a fence with accuracy.

He looked a lot like a gunfighter. Hal noted he had not changed in that respect since the last time they had seen each other four years before. His hat was worn low over his forehead, there was a red bandanna at his neck, which, with his red shirt, showed up well against the black of his long jacket. He carried two Colt 44s, slung low from his belt. He was deeply tanned from the trail and he sported a well-trimmed moustache. His dark eyes were narrow, as if he was forever expecting trouble, and was not afraid to meet it.

Now he rode forward to meet Hal.

'The soldier boy returns!' Ross spoke as if quoting from a song or a poem and there was only the faintest hint of a jeer in his voice. 'Great to see you back, Hal! Slaughtered all them goddamned Rebs single-handed jest about, thet right?'

'Not me,' answered Hal evenly. 'Jest did my share, I guess.'

Ross had not gone to the war. The Clements had not felt strongly about it and there was business to attend to. Part of the time, Ross had been away, attending to things elsewhere, and when the recruitment team had come to Sandstone, he had been detained in cattle-dealing somewhere out West. As the citizens of Sandstone had pointed out, that didn't mean he was yellow, it just meant that – like his old man – he couldn't see any sense in joining the army.

'I ain't here to talk about the war,' went on Hal. 'My father got killed while I was away. The sheriff says your father shot him before a mob decided to hang him.'

'The sheriff's right. That's what happened. You ain't here to look for trouble with my father, I hope? I don't take kindly to any such idea!'

'I want to hear from his own mouth exactly how my father died and why. That ain't too much to ask, is it? Mr Clement at home today?'

'He's out on the range. Anyhow, I don't want any talk about your pa and his hanging. My father won't like it either. It's past. Your old man did somethin' real bad and got what was coming to him when all those townsfolk took their justice.'

'Some justice! Since when is justice given out by a crazy mob? Anyhow, your father put thet first bullet into him and I want to hear it all from his mouth—'

'I told you to let it go, Hal!'

'You weren't there! It's your father I need to speak to.'

'Well, forget it. He has nothing to say. Ask the

goddamned sheriff if you want to know. It's all in his records someplace. I know how sore you feel about this but there's no help for it. Your father messed up thet girl and killed her.' There was the faintest hint of a smirk at the edge of Ross's mouth. 'It ain't your fault if old Billy was getting them kind of ideas in his old age. My father jest stopped him going any further than he already did. Any murder is bad enough but some kinds of murder make you look around for a spittoon.'

Hal sat perfectly still in the saddle. Something told him that Ross Clement thought there was something funny about it all. There was no genuine sympathy for Becky and obvious contempt for Hal's father. It was a story that could be told over a beer and laughed at.

'I don't like your way, Clement,' he heard himself say quietly. He remembered the times he had waited for the signal to charge at the enemy. Always, his nerves had been stretched almost to breaking point. They were like that now – ready to snap. 'My father's dead and can't answer for himself but I hear you loud and clear.'

Ross Clement's hand drifted towards his gunbelt.

'Take it easy, Coburn. We ain't looking for trouble but if you bring it, I guess you'll find it.'

The men at the gate were looking on steadily. They were hard cattlemen, rangy and tough. One man already held a rifle over his saddle-bow. They were all strangers to Hal, except for the one called Bilt. A wrong move from Hal could bring a fusillade of fire and half a dozen witnesses to prove he had drawn first. He nodded slowly and turned the roan back the way he had come.

By the time he rode into Sandstone dusk was falling and lamps were appearing in the windows. Only the saloon was a blaze of light. Groups of men stood on the sidewalk, smoking pipes and drinking from bottles. Most looked at him as he passed and there were grunts of recognition. He heard his name repeated twice but there was no friendly greeting. Eyes caught in the lamplight held a gleam of wary distrust or a hint of defensiveness – sometimes hostility. He rode on without looking to right or left.

When he reached the farm, Blick cooked a meal of bacon and beans with coffee. He had bread too and a few other things.

'You got all this in the store, all right?' asked Hal, smiling for the first time in a long day.

Blick hestitated before replying.

'Not exactly. They wouldn't serve me. Lady went in when she saw me come out and she bought the food with your money. Said her name was Miss Hunter.'

Hal gasped. The storekeeper's attitude did not surprise him too much. That kind of prejudice did not belong only to the far South. It was the lady's name that astonished him. He remembered Liza Hunter – Becky's sister and only relative!

3

Next morning Hal rode out to the Hunter place just about a mile east of Sandstone. It was small and there seemed to be nothing happening on it. The few fields that it possessed had nothing growing but rough grass with a few dairy cattle, which he guessed belonged to another small farmer nearby. The Hunters had not been farmers since the parents died some time before the war. Liza and her young sister had been living alone when he last saw them and at that time she had been earning a modest living as the local schoolteacher. The poverty showed around the place. There were gaps in the fence and moss upon the roof but the little garden at the front was neat and there were clean yellow curtains at the windows.

He hitched the roan at the gate and took his hat off as he went up the narrow path. Before he could knock, the door had opened and she stood there in the porch in a blue dress and white apron. He remembered her as a sixteen-year-old but now she was grown up and womanly, not beautiful exactly, with her dark hair cut a little short and no ornament of any kind, but she was easy on the eye and looked as if she was ready to smile at him if he was pleasant to her.

He did not speak for a moment. In a sense he had been dreading this moment and had thought about it often through the night. A more difficult and awkward situation he could not imagine. He was surprised when she spoke first.

'It's nice to see you back, Mr Coburn. I heard yesterday that you had returned safely. That was really good to know.'

'Thanks, Miss Hunter,' he replied with just a trace of unsteadiness in his voice. 'It's good of you to say so. I am really sorry about Becky. I just heard it when I got back.'

'It was bad for everyone,' she said. He was aware now that her inner tension matched his own. 'Thank you for coming by. I wasn't certain that you would.'

She was looking at him steadily. He knew it was not just the thing for a decent young woman living alone to invite a man into the house but this seemed exceptional. After a little hesitation, she smiled and opened the door wider for him to enter.

As he expected, the room was clean and neat

but with no sign of luxury. There was a picture on the wall of her parents and two female hats on the hallstand one of which, he guessed, had been Becky's. He sat down on a wooden chair by the table while she sat near the window.

'What happened,' she went on, 'could hardly have been worse. I have to live with it and you do too. I know how you must be feeling. Neither of us can help the past and we just have to live on as best we can. It was no one's fault but . . .'

'My father's fault . . . That it?' He tried to keep the bitterness out of his voice but with little success. 'Thing is, I can hardly believe it. My father was a good, gentle kind of a man. It makes no sense to me.'

'It didn't make any sense to anybody at the time. Something just happened to him. It can't be explained. What matters now is going on with life without anger.'

He did not reply at once but sat staring at the floor. He was relieved to know she had come to terms with the tragedy and seemed to have no hatred for her sister's murderer. If she had felt anger before then it had burned itself out. That wasn't the way things were with him. It would take longer than a year or two for him to set all this aside.

'Do you want to tell me what happened?' he asked at last, feeling he had no right to ask it but prompted by an inner need to get at the truth, which he could not yet recognize in the sheriff's story.

But the tale as she told it was about the same as that of Somerville's. It was all second hand, of course. She had been at home all that day when her kid sister had romped out to look for rainbows. In the late afternoon she had learned of Becky's disappearance and had heard of the search-party setting out. Then they had returned with Becky's body and the terrible tale.

'I could hardly believe it,' she finished, a sob coming into her voice for the first time. 'When I saw her little body all covered with that sheet, I thought it must be some ghastly nightmare.'

He did not know what to say. He felt like holding her hand but it was not really possible. Then he pulled himself together, determined to go on a little further with his questioning.

'I know they brought back your sister, which was right, and I'm glad of it, but they left my father hanging. That's hard to take.' He was quiet as the sight of the hanging-tree came back to his mind then he said: 'I've been out there, to Calfskin, but there's nothing left. It's as if he was never there. The rope had been cut but there was nothing at all.'

'I heard that, Hal,' she was using his Christian name for the first time since they had been youngsters. 'Nobody can explain it.'

'Nobody cares, either,' he cut in. 'Somerville isn't interested. He would feel better if I hadn't come back from the war. I can see by the looks of other folks in town that they feel about the same.'

'They feel some guilt, Hal. People don't like that. They have to feel justified in what they do, so I suppose they're ready to face up to you in case you want to blame them.'

'Queer way of thinking, Liza.'

'It's the human way. There's another thing that was strange at the time. You remember Hokay? Well, he came by here the day after on that old mule-cart of his and he shouted that he was sorry about Becky. He didn't stop even when I called to him but just went on by about as fast as the mule could go. He yelled something about it wasn't his fault exactly. The kids had been telling her about the rainbow and he reckoned she would like to see the gold. But he wouldn't stop to explain anything. He shouted something about being scared . . .'

'Scared?'

'That's right. Then he was gone. A couple of days later I heard he had disappeared – just vanished, leaving that shack of his open to the weather. Nobody knew where he went or why.'

Hal remembered Hokay clearly enough. For many years he had lived on a smallholding up near the woods where he grew a few vegetables and made a poor living doing odd jobs about the town. He was an old guy, as Hal had always thought of him, small wiry and wizened-looking with three or four days' stubble always there on his thin face. He remembered Somerville saying something about Hokay filling the girl's head with rubbish about the rainbow and the gold to be found at the end of it.

'You reckon he was scared?'

'He said he was and he looked it. Nobody saw him after that . . . and when he shouted out the word "gold" it sounded like as if perhaps he meant real gold – not just what you might imagine at the foot of the rainbow. Maybe that sounds stupid but there was an emphasis there, easy to pick up.'

Easy for you to pick up, thought Hal. Liza was a smart woman. She had never let up with her reading and trying to educate herself. Even when she was younger it had seemed to him she could sometimes read people like one of her books.

'What did you think of the gold idea?' he asked, already knowing what the answer would be.

'It didn't interest me. I was only thinking about Becky and, later on, a bit worried about Hokay. Folks said he had gone away because he was ashamed of putting that stupid idea into Becky's mind so that she ended up getting murdered.'

The word 'murdered' stabbed again into Hal's heart. There was a weight there that increased

42

every time he heard it. He got up slowly and made for the door.

'Thanks for everything,' he said, without looking at her. 'I had better be on my way.'

'Come again, if you like,' she replied gently. 'We were both hit by the same lightning.'

He rode back through the town, deep in thought. He did not look at the townsfolk who glanced at him as he passed. He knew that every man's face would be likely to fit, in his imagination, into the mob that had surrounded his father. He took a slightly different route to avoid going by the cemetery. On the outskirts he came, to his surprise, on a new building, large and fine-looking. It wasn't quite finished and there were men still working on it.

One of the workmen glanced at him and then stared. Hal stared back in half-recognition. There were a lot of new faces in town since he went away but this one looked vaguely familiar, as if Hal had seen him before in years gone by, maybe on some outlying farm.

'Hey, Hal,' came the voice, rough and dry with dust, 'good to see ya back. Sorry about what happened but I wasn't in it. I was out lookin' for the gal too but I wasn't there when they caught up with your pa. Name's Jesset. Could be ya don't remember me. Anyhow, I reckon it was all too bad.'

'I remember you, all right, Jesset, and you're right about how bad it was and is. But what's all this?'

'New hotel. Mr Clement's place. Reckons there'll be plenty business when the territory opens up with mining and the railroad.'

'No lack of money by the look of it.' Hal nodded with some bitterness. He was in no way concerned about money or the hotel, but the news that Clement was behind it – as in so much else in the region – jarred on his already frayed nerves.

He rode on with Jesset's relieved farewell ringing in his ears. He realized that people were scared in case he was so sore that he might be looking for revenge against somebody. It was the way he felt, sure, but not the way he would act. There was more to this than just a bunch of crazed people. . . .

At about the time Hal stopped to look at the new building, Blick was hammering nails into the broken fencing at the side of the old farmhouse. There were a good many things he could do to help fix the place up and he didn't mind doing any of them. He knew he had been left behind that morning because Hal had personal things to say to the Hunter lady. Blick had already been told about Hal's father and the terrible thing that had happened and it grieved him to think of it. He reckoned that if he did everything possible to help around the farm it might help Hal to feel a bit better.

He was just hammering in the last nail when he heard the sound of hoofs on the stones outside the gate and looked round to see a strange old guy on a mule. The old feller was staring at him with a look of astonishment from behind his grey, straggling beard. Then a row of bad teeth showed from under the moustache.

'Howdy,' came the throaty voice while the rough mass of hair bounced forward in greeting.

'Hya,' replied Blick, grinning as he moved towards the gate. 'What kin I do fer you, Mister?'

'Came to see Hal, to tell ya the truth. He about somewheres?'

'Mr Hal went into town to speak to somebody. Kin I help out?'

'Maybe. You a friend of Hal? I guessed so. I've knowed him too fer a long time. Name's Hokay.'

'Mine's Blick.'

They looked at one another for a moment without speaking. There was a feeling of recognition hanging in the air but nothing to put a name to. It seemed to Blick as if it was like a couple of prairie dogs ready to sit up and chatter and grin but always aware of the need to keep an eye out for the coyotes of this world.

'Didn't expect to see anybody like you,' said Hokay.

'Black do ya mean?' Blick grinned.

'Yeah, black – white – what the hell? Anyways, I came to tell Hal somethin' about his old man. Thing is, I knew Hal was back because I seed him yesterday out near Calfskin though he didn't see me. I keep my head down these days, see, until I'm sure about things. I guessed he was lookin' fer what was left of his pa. Maybe you could tell him thet old Billy got buried proper – did it myself . . .'

'Yeah? How come?'

'How come a little guy like me could shift a big feller like Billy, do ya mean? Well, thing is, I went out with the mule cart thet same night and when I got there, I moved the cart back under old Billy and then climbed up and cut him down. When I got back to where I was goin', I rolled him off and into his grave, thet I had dug previous. It was clumsy but I did it as well as I could. Even read out a bit from the Bible – somethin' about the resurrection. It was as decent as I could make it.'

Blick stared at him in admiration.

'Thet was good of you. Mr Hal will sure be glad to hear thet!'

Hokay seemed pleased and smiled, his face a mass of wrinkles.

'Well, you tell him thet. Another thing, I guess he'll want to visit his pa's grave, so if he comes out to where I'm hiding out, he kin do thet.' Hokay hesitated, feeling he might be taking a chance,

46

then he continued: 'Way out past Magpie Drop there's the woods thet slope down to thet old dried-up river. There's a track thet leads through. Tell Hal it's where his old man met the grizzly. He'll remember thet! Tell him to go by Frazer Gulch which is the long way round – not direct – 'cause there are white Injuns around thet want to take my scalp. I came by Frazer, myself, and kept my head down all the way. Being here right now is as risky as hell but I had to tell Hal about his old man. Now I'm goin' to git back! Remember and tell Hal everything. I'll know when he's comin' and I'll see him before he sees me.'

Hokay stopped speaking and looked at Blick closely.

'You're an easy guy to talk to. Generally, I don't find folks easy thet way. Mostly they make me feel as if I've jest crawled out of the swamp . . .'

'I know the feeling,' Blick replied with a grin.

He watched as Hokay rode off back the way he had come. The mule could move pretty quickly for a draught animal and it was soon out of sight. Blick whistled as he sauntered back to the house. It was a bit of good news for Hal – about as good as any news about his father's grave could be in the circumstances.

Hal returned not long after Hokay's departure. The news of his father's burial brought a sense of relief, however rough it had had to be. He made up his mind that he must visit the grave but resisted the temptation to follow Hokay too soon. From Blick's explanations, he realized that it would be unwise. If danger existed for Hokay as he had stated, then to follow immediately on his trail would be more likely to attract attention and increase the danger.

Early next morning he and Blick set off on horseback with the idea of taking the long route as suggested by Hokay. Hal knew the way pretty well. Frazer Gulch was well known but seemed to point the wrong way as far as getting to the vicinity of Magpie Drop was concerned. The trail through it was narrow and the rocky, scrub-covered sides gave good cover. It was long, though, and hard enough going, but at length they came to where the woods took over from the stony landscape. They skirted the stands of pine and deciduous trees until Hal saw the track that he remembered from his boyhood. This was where his father had narrowly escaped death from the bear all those years ago. That was still fresh in his memory.

The trail through the woods was little more than a deer track and seemed almost unused but Hal saw, here and there, signs of recent passage in the shape of broken twigs and crushed bracken. The sweet smell of the forest hung in the air and there was a stillness that caught at his breath. His mind went back to such cautious advances he and his comrades had made through the woodlands of the South, always broken by rifle-fire and death. Here he did not expect that but Hokay's warning to Blick made him very careful and he remained alert and watchful with every yard of progress.

Even so, he was taken by surprise when Hokay appeared from behind the trees and held up a cheerful hand in greeting. He said nothing but gestured with a rifle carried under his arm for them to follow him further into the undergrowth. There was barely enough room for the horses to make their way but in a short time they reached a clearing where Hokay called a halt in a subdued tone and signalled for them to dismount.

Here the ground had been cleared and a stretch of earth showed, flat except for a scattering of stones. Hokay glanced at Hal and then took off his hat.

'Here's Billy's grave,' he said simply. 'The best I could do.'

Hal stood still, aware of a mixture of emotion flowing through him. To be brought to actual evidence of his father's death somehow struck him to the heart. In a way, it seemed even worse than seeing the grave of his mother, which at least had been in the churchyard and not in the lonely woods He was grateful, just the same, that there had been a burial and he had seen no bones of his father lying in the dirt.

'I didn't put up a cross or anythin',' went on Hokay. 'Every once in a while some guy lookin' to trap critters comes around here and could git curious. This way, he would likely think it was jest the marks left by an old Injun hogan and go on by.'

'Yeah, good idea,' replied Hal. 'I'm real grateful, Hokay. My father shouldn't ever have been left hanging on that tree. Nobody deserves that!'

He glanced sharply at Hokay who was scratching his nose and looking at him sideways. It was as if the old feller had something else on his mind.

'What else, Hokay? This trip out here ain't jest to see the grave, is it. I would have come for that reason anyhow but what else are you thinking about?'

'Thing is, Hal,' came the hesitant reply. 'Well, I was never sure whether to say this – 'cause ya could hold me to account too – but I knowed all along thet old Billy didn't ever kill thet gal, though I ain't never had the guts to say so. He never did it and he never drew on Pete Clement either. It was all lies and Billy got blamed and was killed off before he could say any different.'

Hal did not move. It was as if he had been struck over the back of the head with a stick. He felt stunned. Then he stared hard at Hokay.

'You'd better tell me. I need to know,' he said at last, his voice sounding hollow.

'All right, Hal. Thing is . . .'

There came a faint crack from somewhere behind and Hal whirled round to see a figure vanishing into the bushes. Blick bounded forward, his long legs shortening the distance in seconds. He caught up with the man and brought him to the ground with a crash. There was swift struggle and the man half-rose, a knife flashing in his hand. Then Hokay's rifle boomed.

When they reached the spot where Blick was rising to his feet, they found the corpse of a man with black hair and dressed in a leather jacket lying in the bracken. He looked dark-skinned and wore a bone ornament through his ear. A half-drawn gun protruded from his belt.

'Feller must have been on your trail, sure enough,' grunted Hokay. 'Half-breed cowhand. Sharp as a razor when it comes to tracking.' He glanced at Hal, worry in his eyes. 'One of Clement's men – I kin tell ya thet for certain. Means he's keeping a sharp look-out fer you as well as me . . .'

4

They found the man's pony near the deer track and Hokay took it in hand, saying he would release it a few miles away where somebody would find it and think it had strayed. He promised also to make sure that the dead cowhand would not be found. He led the pony and his two friends back through the woods, not to the grave, but to another clearing about quarter of a mile further on where he said he had his little abode.

It turned out to be an old Indian hogan, half-sunk in the earth, covered with branches and birch-bark, and showing signs of recent repair.

'Ain't much of a place,' he admitted, but it does me jest fine. I been livin' out here fer a good while. When it comes to trappin' rabbits and squirrels and catchin' fish from the stream, there ain't anybody better . . .'

'What is it you're scared of?' asked Hal. 'Pete Clement? What's this really all about, Hokay? And what about my father? Let's have it!'

Hokay looked at him sharply and nodded. He then motioned for them both to accompany him into the gloom of the hogan. There seemed nothing inside but a rough bed and a cooking-pot. They crouched in the half-dark as there was no room to stand up straight.

'Well, I better tell ya now,' said Hokay. 'Thing is, I've always had it in mind thet ya might come back from the war and maybe thet's why I never lit straight out of the territory while the goin' was good. I guess I always felt ya needed to know.'

Hal curbed his impatience, his mouth pursing.

Hokay was lifting a small reed mat in the corner of the hut. Under it, Hal caught sight of the wooden lid of a box. Then Hokay opened it and both Hal and Blick gasped as the glint of gold reflected the faint light from the door. Hokay lifted out a gold bar.

'There's five of them,' he said casually. 'About three years ago there was a robbery from the Fletcher mine over at Carey Bight about forty miles from here. These three guys must have come riding like hell with the loot over towards Sandstone but the US marshal caught up with them. There was a shoot-out and they was all killed but nobody ever found the gold. Then . . .' Hokay hesitated, licking his lips and pondering, as if he could still see it all in his mind, 'one day, I was goin' through by Calfskin Rock and I came to the bit where there's a gully and I sees a board stickin' out from the sand. I guess it had been uncovered by the wind thet day which was pretty fierce. When I looked close I saw the gold and knew right away what I had found. So I covered it over again and put a few rocks on top to keep it safer. I reckoned it was as good a place as any.'

'You thought about returning it to the mine or the sheriff?' suggested Hal.

'Never did. Thing is, I reckoned if I did thet, all I would git out of it would be a slap on the back and a ten-dollar tip. Folks don't ever see no sense in givin' money to a muskrat like me. Thet right, Blick? Guys like us is supposed to live on fresh air and handouts. So I kept it a secret and thought maybe I could go off sometime and be a rich man somewhere else. Only I could never imagine me trying to sell a gold bar to a bank or somebody without the sheriff being called in right away. So I did nothin' but wait. Mind you, it was funny to think of folks handin' me a few cents for painting a back door or somethin' and them never knowin' thet I was the richest man in the land!'

Hokay chuckled and winked at Blick.

'All right, but what about my father?' snapped Hal, his patience wearing thin.

'I'm comin' to it,' said Hokay. 'Bit more than a year ago we had a couple of rainy days in the

54

middle of the summer. I was in Sandstone with the mule and I hears the kids laughin' and goin' on about gold at the foot of the rainbow and, sure enough, there was a fine rainbow thet seemed to stretch all over the sky. Becky was there too and she seemed to believe it. Next thing I knew, she was running out of the town saying she was goin' to find the gold. I didn't pay much attention at first and jest went on working at a bit of the sidewalk thet had come loose. After a while, though, I got a bit worried at the thought of thet harum-scarum gal running off without nobody thinking about her and I got on the mule and went after her. Caught up with her way out in the country, still aiming fer that goddamned rainbow end.

'Well, I told her to git up on the mule behind me and it was then I gits one of my crazy ideas. Ya know, Blick, about them crazy notions. Bet you git them too!' He glanced at Blick again, who shrugged his shoulders and grinned. Crazy ideas weren't exactly his style but he could see it all in Hokay. 'Anyhow, I thinks it would be one hell of a joke if I really did show her some gold supposed to be at the end of the rainbow, so we rode on out towards Calfskin with her and me talkin' and laughin' all the way. She was real easy to speak to, I kin tell ya. Better then anybody I ever met. When we got there, I left the mule and took Becky down the gully and opened up the gold. Ya should have seen her face! It was a picture!

'But then I thought maybe this was a big mistake 'cause as sure as hell she would tell everybody in town about it and somebody would believe it, so I covers the box again and took her up to the mule and told her it had to be our secret. Jest then, I hears somebody hollerin' some distance away and Becky leaves go of my hand and says she wants to see the gold again and runs down the gully again before I could stop her and kicks the stones aside and pulls open the lid. Then I saw old Billy, your pa, on the slope at the other side of the gully. He was on his mare and there was a pronghorn at his saddle, so I knew he had been out shootin'. He jest stared at Becky and I was jest about to call out to him when Pete Clement appeared at the top of the gully on horseback. When he saw Becky, he dismounted quick as a flash, and then looked amazed as he saw the gold which was all gleaming in the sun after the rains.

'Then somethin' terrible happened.' Hokay paused for a moment as if he could not go on. 'Then the gal ran up the slope towards Pete Clement, yelling about the gold, and he put out his hand as if to stop her to ask about it and caught her arm and she spun round and fell back head first into the gully. She jest lay there and I could see from where I was high up there in the rocks thet her neck was broke.'

'I didn't move. I wasn't able to. It was like a hell of a shock. Then Pete drew his gun and shot Billy and I hid myself better and put my hat over the mule's nose to stop it snorting 'cause I knew thet I would be next if Pete saw me. I watched, though, as Pete scrambled down the slope and covered up the gold and then I saw a horrible thing as he took off Billy's belt and put it round the gal's neck as if she had been strangled by it. But there were more folks comin'. I could hear them yelling out Becky's name but she, poor kid, couldn't answer, and I went off, quiet as a deer, 'cause I knew there was terrible trouble and I couldn't get mixed in it.'

'You didn't stay to tell them folks what had happened?' asked Hal, amazed.

'Nope. Maybe I should have but it was Pete Clement I was facing and who would believe me instead of him? Next day I heard about what they all did to Billy and the yarn thet Pete Clement had invented. Everybody believed it, even the sheriff so I kept my mouth shut. But I went out at night and took away your pa and the gold and came way out here and buried him as decent as I could. Then I went back into town and went about my business jest exactly as normal. After thet, I heard Bilt Cameron had been out to Calfskin and came back to tell the sheriff thet Billy's body had gone. Somerville didn't seem to do much about it and Judge Elder couldn't figure it out either although he reckoned it had been taken away and buried by somebody with a bit of conscience. He was kind of mad about the lynching though he didn't look into it too closely. Probably thought it would be too goddamned complicated to sort out – so thet seemed to be the end of it and nobody knew anything about the gold except me and I couldn't decide what to do about thet! Until a feller called Jesset told me one day thet Pete Clement wanted to see me – somethin' about gold at the end of the rainbow – only I knew it wasn't no rainbow! Pete must have been thinking pretty hard or maybe one of his Injun cowhands had seen me out near Calfskin with the mule – so I decided to clear out. I didn't fancy no interview with Pete Clement if he had gold in his mind!'

He fell silent and no one spoke for some minutes. Blick stared thoughtfully at the hogan wall. Hal was tense. His face was set in a mask of anger as he thought of Pete Clement gunning down his father. He knew he would settle with the murdering snake as soon as he could make the opportunity. All this, though, ought to have been done before now. Clement, by rights, should have been hanged long since. Billy Coburn ought to have been treated with honour as the decent man he always had been.

'Hokay,' he said at last, keeping a firm grip on his emotions, 'my father – your old friend, Billy –

was shot down in cold blood. You saw it happen! You knew he was innocent of any crime! But you never spoke out for him. If you had it might have gone the other way . . . Why?'

'I told ya why, Hal.' Hokay sounded suddenly hurt and wounded at Hal's tone, but there was guilt in his voice for the first time. 'I ain't nothin' around here or anywhere else. It was my word against Clement's. Who do ya think would be believed – me or a big-shot rancher like him? Then, after I had spoke out, what do ya think would have happened? My life wouldn't have been worth a plugged nickel, thet's fer sure!'

There was truth in that. If Hokay had made such an accusation and had been disbelieved, the chances of his survival in the face of Clement's fury would have been slim. Hal put out a hand and pressed it on Hokay's shoulder.

'All right, I see what you mean. Thanks a million for at least burying old Billy.' He got up and stooped as he went outside the low door. 'I got the rest of this business to clear up. . . .'

He led the roan through the trees back towards the deer track with Blick following. They were silent for a long time as they rode back the way they had come by way of the gulch and the woodlands. Hal's mind was full of hatred for Pete Clement and, in his imagination, he saw himself shoot down the rancher as he had been forced many times before to shoot at men he did not know and hardly felt to be his enemies.

'Mr Hal.' Blick's voice came from behind, penetrating his thoughts by its urgency. 'You reckon on settling this whole thing with Pete Clement at the end of your gun-sight?'

'That's jest about the way I see it, sure enough,' said Hal. 'How else?'

'Oughta be done legal, if you ask me. If it comes to a gunfight over this then whose to blame for it – you or him?'

'Him . . . if there's any justice.'

Hal was silent for a long time. He recognized the impossibility of obtaining justice in any gunfight with Pete Clement over this. As far as the law was concerned the right man had been hanged for a terrible crime committed. Not hanged according to law, certainly, but it was done anyway and nobody would be looking to reopen the case.

'Maybe Hokay could tell the sheriff what really happened.' Blick broke the silence as if their earlier conversation was still in progress. 'He saw the whole thing. He's a hot-shot witness, ain't he?'

'Sure, but who's goin' to believe him – especially after all this time? He was right about Clement being listened to before a guy like himself. Hokay has no influence. Folks think he's jest some kind of a crazy buzzard who's always jest making stories up

– like the rainbow yarn that led to all the trouble in the first place!'

It was evidence of some desperation rising in Blick's mind that he could suggest that Somerville might believe Hokay. Hal knew what was prompting the feeling. Blick did not want this fight between Clement and his friend. It could only mean disaster for Hal even if he walked away unharmed and left his opponent sprawled out dead on the ground. He would have become an outlaw, for the law would see no justification for it. It would look like an act of revenge just because his criminal father had been shot down before he could kill for a second time.

It seemed that public justice was not to be had. Hal set his mouth in bitter anger and frustration. It was as if the world had suddenly emptied itself of all meaning. All through the war he had dreamed of returning to Sandstone Creek and living a decent and worthwhile life thereafter but it had been an idle hope, for the bear-pit had already been dug for him and he could not avoid it. He knew there was no way he could live in the shadow of such an injustice as had been suffered by his father – old Billy, as innocent a man as had ever lived.

Pete Clement had to pay. That seemed certain. It must mean an end to his own hopes of living the life of a decent citizen and it could well mean the end of his own existence but there seemed no other course. Clement, the cold-blooded killer, could not be left alive to enjoy his victory over a good and quiet man who had done no harm but whose name had been blackened in the worst possible way.

'Miss Hunter. You goin' to see her, Mr Hal?'

'Sure thing, Blick, on our way back now.'

She was in the front garden when they arrived in the late afternoon. One lock of hair hung over her forehead and she had in her hands a small bunch of yellow flowers. She smiled as they drew rein at her gate but she had an air of expectancy as she stared at them.

He told her about Hokay as they stood there in the open air. There was no one within earshot and it seemed quite safe. When he explained how Becky had actually died, she drew in her breath and for a moment they held hands. It seemed a natural gesture and it was done without thought. When she realized it she withdrew her hand but with a slow tenderness.

'Come into the house,' she suggested. 'You both look as if you need something to drink. I have coffee or mineral water.'

As they were seated, she expressed her gratitude for the news being brought so quickly and then remained silent for a few minutes as they drank. It was as if she waited on a decision.

'I am happier, much happier,' she said at last, 'to know that Becky wasn't murdered. She died a violent death but not with the fear and suffering I have always thought.' She looked at the floor. 'You know how it was, Hal, everything I was told . . . What else could I believe? It always seemed like madness to think of your father . . .'

'Attacking Becky?' Hal filled in the rest of her sentence as she hesitated. 'Sure, there was nothing else for you to think. Anyway, it didn't happen like that. It was bad enough, sure, but at least it was quick. I guess she didn't know all that much about it.'

'And it means your father was innocent. That's a wonderful thing to know! We must see the sheriff. Pete Clement needs to be brought to justice!'

'It means bringing in Hokay but he can't testify without incriminating himself. He has stayed silent all this time and he still has the gold. Looks like trying to help the murderer and to steal the loot from that robbery.'

'Yes, but your father's name must be cleared. They might not be too hard on Hokay . . . him being the way he is.'

Hal nodded faintly but was unconvinced. They might be as hard as hell on Hokay – if he was believed. If he wasn't then he might be ignored by the law but Clement wouldn't forget.

'Let's see the sheriff now,' put in Liza. 'We'll all

go. He must listen to us. Then we'll bring in Hokay.'

Liza was persuasive when she had made up her mind. Hal knew it was something that had to be tried anyway but found it hard to believe that Somerville would take action.

He was right. The sheriff received the trio with some surprise and stared at Hal in trepidation, obviously expecting trouble. He treated Liza with the respect due to a lady but there was no genuine welcome for any of them. He listened with an expression of increasing astonishment as Hal outlined the story as told by Hokay and his eyes took on a particularly startled look at the mention of the gold, but he shook his head slowly as if in disbelief.

'This Hokay guy, well I ask you, Hal, how much confidence can you have in him? Always lived more or less like a hobo and half-crazy too! All thet stuff about rainbows and gold! It was him thet got thet poor gal all mad and runnin' off and gettin' herself . . . Sorry, Miss Hunter, but you know what happened well as I do now! You can't put no store in anything he says!'

'I've seen the gold,' said Hal bluntly.

'Yeah, well, thet's as may be, but if Hokay found any gold, specially if it's thet stuff from the robbery, then it should be returned right away. He ought to have done thet at the start! Where's he hiding it? I'll git some men together and go and collect it.' He was silent for a brief moment, thinking of the advantage to himself if he could bring in the gold lost by the company for over a year. 'You say he definitely has it?'

'What really matters, Sheriff Somerville,' put in Liza, in a controlled voice, 'is bringing the killer of Mr Coburn to justice. It is high time we were dealing with that murderer and clearing Hal's father's name in this town.'

'But, Miss Hunter, it was your sister . . . You surely don't believe now thet this story is true?'

'I do believe it. It makes more sense than the one everybody in this town has believed all this time. It may be hard for people to accept how wrong they have been but it needs to be done. You're the sheriff here. You should bring Pete Clement in for questioning.'

It was the one thing Somerville did not want to do. He was afraid to do it. Hal could see it in the man's eyes. Clement was too dangerous and had men of his own kind ready to back him up. He smiled faintly and bitterly. It was exactly as he had expected. There was to be no help from the law in this matter.

'Let's go,' he said, standing up and putting on his hat. 'Some people are only good for chewing the fat and filling in their notebooks.'

They rode back in the dusk to Liza's place. She

was silent as if she could not help but agree with him. They parted company at her gate and she held on to his hand for another brief moment. It was as if there was some feeling between them which had been there for a long time – since they were children – but had remained unrecognized until now. Blick stared through the half-dark. If his features had been visible they would have recorded surprise, embarrassment and pleasure. His teeth gleamed in his familiar grin but then dropped into concern as the other thought struck him. . . .

Hal and Blick did not talk as they rode through the darkness towards home. Both were busy with their thoughts. Hal felt confused. The understanding which had suddenly sprung up between himself and Liza made him feel like shouting out for joy but it was ruined by what he knew lay in front of him. Somerville would do nothing, which meant that he, Hal, must see to Clement himself. It was to be as he had guessed all along. There could be no future with Clement alive and no future with Liza when Hal, himself, was branded as the rancher's killer.

The silence between Hat and Blick continued as they came into the farm and stabled the horses. Blick knew what was in Hal's mind but said nothing. At length Hal spoke, his voice controlled but not quite covering his inner tension.

'Well, I'm going to make something out of this farm, Blick. It's in poor shape with all the neglect but we can build it up again. Tomorrow, I'll ride over to Pierceville for seed. That's the best place to git it. Maybe you can do something with that old chicken-coop.'

His words suggested he had given up all thought of looking for justice for his father. Blick knew that wasn't the case. Hal had decided to bide his time. He would carry on as a small-time farmer until Clement dropped his guard – as he would do – sometime. There would come a day when the rancher would consider Hal to be no longer a threat, having been forced to accept the situation. The rancher would ride into town, maybe to visit that new hotel of his. Then Hal would act. The challenge would be issued, guns drawn, and the matter settled once and for all. That might be a bad day for Pete Clement, thought Blick, but it would be the end for Hal.

In the morning, Hal set off early for Pierceville. Blick watched him go, his usual grin no longer in evidence. Then he went to begin work on the old chicken-coop. As he straightened out the rusty wire and searched around for newer posts to replace the rotten ones, he felt he was wasting his time. This idea of putting the farm into working order was more of a sham than a reality. It was

designed to fool Clement, not as a means of building a future for Hal, much less Hal and Liza. He
worked hard just the same, as was his way, and was
fully absorbed in the task when Hokay arrived with
no more noise than a deer.

'Hey, Blick.' The lined face seemed even more
screwed up than usual and the voice was low and
husky. 'Thought I'd better look you up this
mornin'. Hal around?'

'Nope. He's gone away to some place called
Pierceville for seed.'

'Yeah? Gittin' back to serious farmin', is he? I
bet!'

They looked at one another, both understanding, then Hokay spat on the ground.

'You had a talk with Somerville, thet right? He
ain't goin' to do anything about Clement. Yeah, I
thought it would be that way. The only thing thet
no-good sheriff might be interested in would be
the gold. He'll be coming around here pretty soon
again to find out where I am so that he kin check
for sure if I've got it or not. I guess you and Hal
ain't planning to tell him?'

'No, sirree, Hokay. We won't never do that!'

'Still, I'm gittin' to feel like a coon with the
hounds sniffing nearer than ever. It's all got to
change.' He fell silent and watched as Blick
hammered a length of chicken-wire on to a post,
then he said: 'You ain't really expecting thet wire

to hold in no chickens, are you?'

'Guess not, Hokay.'

'Me and you kin look into the goddamned future like a couple of them magic owls the Indians used to listen to out in the woods. Hal will wait until Clement thinks he's too busy with his chickens and stuff to notice and walks out into the open, then it will be show-down time and Hal will either git shot or hanged, depending on how it goes on the day, thet right?'

'You got it.'

'It ain't no good, Blick.'

'There ain't no arguing with Mr Hal, when he makes up his mind. Anyhow, I can see where he's coming from. I'd be looking to settle things with Clement myself, if I was in the same situation . . .'

'Straight shootin' ain't always the best way. Sometimes the wrong guys git killed. In this case, if Clement or his side-kicks don't shoot Hal then the law will hang him. Thet's for sure. Be a lot better if it never comes to that. Maybe Clement could die of lead poisoning without Hal being mixed up in it at all.'

'How come?'

'Bushwhacking.'

Blick stopped hammering and stared. He dropped the hammer on the ground and whistled.

'What about bushwhacking, Hokay? It sure ain't Mr Hal's way. He always fights fair and square.'

'So he does thet and it all ends up as we jest said. He'll be a dead man, you'll be left here with the chicken-wire and thet fine gal goes on teaching in the school.' He shrugged his shoulders beneath his ragged jacket and snorted through his beard. 'I ain't much of a romantic but I've always known thet these two had a notion for one another. This way there's no future for either of them. Bushwhacking kin fix it because it'll settle Pete Clement without Hal drawing a gun!'

Blick considered as he picked up his hammer. The idea seemed to make some sense if it could be made to work although it seemed like murder. Only killing a man who was a murderer himself could be regarded as lawful execution.

'You got something in mind, Hokay?' he asked.

'Sure, I've been figuring it out. We need to git old Clement out in the open. The gold might do that. See, if you went up to the Clement place and made out you were sick and tired of working for Hal and were looking to do a deal with the gold so as to clear out of here and live your own life then he might be drawn out. The gold could be put someplace as bait. You lead Clement to it and I bushwhack him.'

'Reckon you kin do that?'

'Yeah. Tell you what, there's a place where I kin lay low and git him clear as a coon in the backyard. See, when you leave the Clement place lead him

70

and whoever he takes along by the west trail for about three miles, then cut off by the track through the woods. After a while, you'll come out to a clear stretch and you'll see a big granite boulder up ahead. There's plenty of other stones around there but keep your eye on the big hunk of granite with the sharp edge. When you git to the edge you'll see my cart with the gold.'

'You're really bringing the gold?'

'Well, it ain't never been any good to me. Anyhow, when you see the cart, set spurs to your horse and make for the trees just up ahead. Clement and his party will be looking too hard at the gold to try to stop you. Thet's exactly where I'll bring him down. It's risky for you, sure enough, but we need to git all this mess sorted out before Hal jumps in at the deep end.'

'Risky for you too, ain't it?'

'I got the perfect set-up for a bushwhacking. They won't find me and you'll have a pretty good start on them. Head south into the deeper timber and then lie low. In the middle of the night I'll come through the woods calling like a nightjar and let you know we're in the clear.'

It all sounded a bit crazy to Blick. There were plenty of things that might go wrong with it but at least it was a plan that might just work out.

'What do ya say, Blick?'

'All right. When?'

'Saturday next. Old man Clement is always at home on Saturdays counting out money for his men's wages. Go early in the morning. I'll wait until noon and if you don't come by then I'll creep away like a coyote and we kin try somethin' else another time. Need to keep Hal out of it, though!'

'Sure, I kin see that. So we'll try it. See ya noon on Saturday . . .'

'You got it wrong already! See you around midnight. Nobody sees me at noon!'

Hokay vanished as quietly as he had arrived. Blick shook his head thoughtfully. It was the kind of crazy idea he might have expected from Hokay but he could not think of a better one to keep Hal out of Boot Hill. Well, there was one other way. It might come to that yet but he would try Hokay's plan first . . .

Blick was still working when Hal returned in the afternoon. Not much was said for Hal's depression was evident. Over the next couple of days, Blick was as cheerful as he could manage and kept his nerves under control as Friday night approached. He did not sleep at all that night. Before the sun rose, he crept from the house and led the mare silently through the dark. He did not saddle her, fearing to make any sound. When he felt it was safe, he mounted and rode bareback. In his belt he carried the old Navy pistol he had retained from his service days. He glanced back only once in the direction of the farm and sighed, his grin now quite gone.

He had the feeling he might not return.

5

Ross Clement was in a foul mood. His thin lips were tight behind his neat moustache and he scowled as he leaned over the wooden fence in the morning air and gazed unseeing over the field where his father's milk cattle grazed.

On any other morning he would have eaten breakfast with his father but today he felt he could not have tolerated any more of his old man's talk about the ranching and the swell place that had been built up over the years and the fine future that lay ahead for his son if he would only apply himself and continue his father's work – a much easier task considering the strong foundation already existing.

That much was true, sure, about the powerful springboard for the future in place in the shape of the ranch and its riches. That, however, did not cut much ice with Ross whose ambition lay elsewhere; in one of the great cities, for instance, where a man with money could forge ahead without the dirt and smell and boredom of working with cattle – all of which filled Ross with intense dissatisfaction.

The argument the evening before had been fiercer than ever, so much so that Ross had not breakfasted with his father as he usually did, but had drunk a mug of coffee only before walking out of the house. There were other things on his mind too, such as that girl he had met near Catfish Drift and the other in the city of Sheridan. There was nothing like them around here. It seemed there were only farmers' daughters, smelling like sheep-dip, and straight-laced school-marms and Sunday-school teachers.

His old man, just the same, wouldn't look at things his way and there was no more money forth-coming for Ross to go wandering off to the better life. Old Pete wanted his son to get himself ready for taking over the ranch business and there was no prospect of selling any part of it to make ready cash to fulfil Ross's ambitions, such as they were.

Not that Pete Clement was a model citizen who had built up a sound business only on hard work and enterprise. Ross was well aware that there were things in his father's life which would have set lawmen bringing out their handcuffs after a first gasp of surprise. He knew about the gold stolen from the Fletcher mine which had gone missing after the shoot-out with the US marshal years ago. Pete had been mixed up in that and in fact had been the brains behind the robbery which his underlings had botched and paid for with their lives. The loss of the gold had been a bitter pill for Pete to swallow and he had cursed these dead men for their incompetence. Only the accidental sight of it on the day when he had got mixed up in the search for Becky Hunter had given him a sense of relief – but that had been short-lived.

Ross knew about the girl's death, how it had really happened, and the death of old Billy Coburn, which had been plain murder to silence a man who had suddenly come to know too much. Pete had told Ross the story a couple of times when he was loose-tongued with whiskey, something which was becoming too habitual for comfort. Not, of course, that Ross was in any way shocked at cold-blooded murder. He had been guilty of that himself in the past but he was beginning to see that old Pete might not keep the lid on the story for very much longer.

Would that be such a bad thing? Ross had turned the idea over in his mind a few times in his nights of discontent. If his father vanished for some reason what would be the point of staying on to waste his life in ranching when so much money could be released for better things?

'Hey, Mr Clement, black feller down at the outer

gate wants to come in!' The guard, hurrying up the path, had difficulty in keeping a grin from his freckled young face at the same time as the slight hesitation in his voice indicated a nervousness at disturbing the younger of the two bosses, who looked in a morose frame of mind at that early hour of the morning. 'What do I do? Kick him on his way or what?'

Ross looked surprised. Visitors early in the day were unusual – black ones unknown. He considered for a moment, then he shrugged and accompanied the guard down the long pathway. He was aware of a sense of curiosity. Black guy, heh? An idea was coming into his mind. He had heard of a coloured man coming to the town, hadn't he? Of course, Hal Coburn's man – that was it! Jesus, what was this about? The young Coburn had had the look of a mad wolf the last time he had been around here. He needed to be kept at bay. What did he think he could accomplish by sending his man to the ranch on some errand?

At the foot of the long drive Blick sat on the saddle-less mare with his thumping heart well hidden by the brilliant smile which disguised his feelings. He was under the gaze of the other guard, bearded and stern, who stared at him as if he had just sprung out of a gooseberry bush. Under his shirt, Blick could feel the hardness of the Navy pistol. It gave him no comfort because it seemed to be marking out the end of his life as it imprinted itself on his naked skin.

He had come for Pete Clement and if it didn't work out one way it must be made to work out in another.

He tried not to breathe too heavily. It was necessary that he should appear calm. He knew that Hokay's plan could go all wrong. Clement might not fall for the bait or Hokay's sharp-shooting might not be as good as he imagined. It was a situation in which Blick was likely to take a bullet as he was caught in an act of treachery. Clement would not stand about waiting for an explanation. It could all go to hell, easy as pie!

There was always the chance, however, that it might work out. If it did not, then Blick had resolved to attempt to kill Pete Clement himself. That was why the Navy pistol was stuck in his belt under his shirt. If Blick killed Pete Clement then Hal would live and have a good life. Otherwise Hal would get killed with a bullet or finish up on the end of a rope. Blick had known that ever since the meeting with Hokay at the hogan and the need to do something about it had been with him since he saw Hal and Liza together in the dusk of the evening.

Not that Blick was much more of a romantic than was Hokay, but he could not see the best friend he had ever known finish up dead and in disgrace without trying to help out. If that meant the end of himself, well too bad. Hal was ready to give up his life for the memory of his wronged father and it did not seem to Blick that he could do less for Hal. In any case, there was a feeling in Blick that he had already left a chunk of himself somewhere out on the battlefield with his comrades who had died with a greater sense of freedom than they had ever known throughout most of the years of their lives. He knew that if he ever saw Hal lying dead he must shoot the man responsible no matter what the inevitable consequence for himself. It was better to switch all that right round so that some good could come of it . . . so it seemed to him.

Ross was looking hard at him, waiting for his strange visitor to speak.

'Come to see Mr Clement,' explained Blick with a grin.

'Thet's me. I'm Clement.'

'Needs to be the older Mr Clement,' said Blick, remembering what he had heard of the family. 'I got news for him. Bit of a surprise.'

'You can tell me.'

'Nope. This is about the older Mr Clement's gold.'

'Gold?'

'Yeah. The gold thet appeared at the end of the rainbow and then slid all the way up to the sky again. I found the other end of the same rainbow.'

'You nuts?'

'Nope, jest lucky.'

Clement jerked his head as a signal that the guards should move out of earshot The less they heard of the conversation the better. He drew his pistol and pointed it at Blick.

'How come you know something about gold? Better talk fast. I ain't a patient man.'

'So I heard, but I'm talking only to Mr Clement – senior! It's his gold. Leastways, he thinks so.'

Ross thought for a moment of carrying out his threat. He was in no mood to listen to half-crazy Negroes and he did not like the suggestion that he was less important than his father But there was something about this man that indicated he was not scared of bullets at the present time.

'All right, but get down off the horse. I'm on foot so you'd better be too.'

They walked slowly up the long path towards the house. Blick was a little surprised to see how fine it looked at close quarters but he gave no sign of being impressed. The door was opened as they approached and Pete Clement appeared, his lank, grey hair hanging over his forehead, his sharp features twisted into a scowl. He glanced at his son and opened his mouth as if to continue their argument of the night before, then he stared at Blick.

'Who the hell's this? Don't remember inviting no black fellers!'

'This here's Hal Coburn's man. Wants to tell you something about gold.'

Pete stood in surprised silence for a moment. He had heard of Hal Coburn coming back from the war with a black man to work for him. He had heard too that Hal had been to see the sheriff a couple of nights ago and he had waited with some anxiety to hear from Somerville himself what it was all about. He knew it must have something to do with old Billy and the dead girl but did not believe anything much would come of it. Young Coburn could squeal all he liked but all that business was wrapped up and if Coburn wanted to make something out of it and started reaching for his guns, he would be on the wrong side of the law and would suffer the consequences in double-quick time. Nevertheless, Pete had been on his guard and kept his armed men on hand.

'Where's Hal Coburn?' he asked abruptly.

'Gone to a place called Pierceville,' answered Blick with convincing alacrity. 'Wants to buy seed and stuff. Reckons on dragging thet rundown place up by its bootlaces,' he added with a deliberate trace of contempt.

'Yeah? So what's all this bull about the gold? What gold? I don't know anything about gold,' growled Pete.

'Well now, see here, Mr Clement, there's a feller called Hokay who reckons you found some a long time ago but he took it and held on to it. Now he says it ain't never been any use to him and reckons on making a deal with yourself. He says it needs to be you because you've always had a special interest and he knows you won't go to the law because there were things happening around that time that are better not talked about. Thet's jest what he told me. He won't deal with nobody but you. He's waiting to see you right now, with the gold standing by.'

Pete stared for a long moment. He had always had some suspicion of Hokay mostly because of all that talk about gold at the end of the rainbow but also because of Hokay's sudden disappearance. Pete had at the time detailed a few men to search around for him but without result and he had eventually concluded that Hokay had left the territory altogether. Many a night he had spent turning over in his mind the possibility that the gold had gone along with the half-crazed old goat This was the first confirmation he had ever had that he had been at least partly right.

'What do you get out of this?' Pete growled at last.

'Fifty dollars from Hokay.'

'That all? What are we talking about here – all the gold or just some of it?'

'All of it. Hokay still has it all intact. Fifty dollars might not seem much to you, but it's more money than I've ever seen. I kin start a whole new life with fifty dollars!'

'You searched this guy, Ross? No! Here Joe!' Pete called to a man standing at a corner of the building. 'See if this feller's armed!'

In a trice Blick's pistol had been taken from his belt and the shirt stripped from his body. His heart sank at finding himself disarmed. He had always reckoned on killing Clement himself if Hokay's plan went haywire but there was no chance of that now.

'What's to stop me putting a bullet into your belly right now,' snarled Pete. 'I might just do that if you don't tell me where the gold is! We could give you a whipping and take that grin off your face!'

'No chance,' grinned Blick. He swung round to show his scarred back. 'I've had too many whip-pings to let them worry me . . . and I ain't scared of death neither. Seen too much of it,' he added, with truth. 'If you kill me you get nothing.'

Pete Clement could see the sense in that. If the gold was really to be had then this feller seemed to offer the only chance of getting it . . . if he could be trusted.

'Where did you say Hal Coburn is today?'

'Pierceville, like I said. Gone to get stuff for his

place. Thinks he can make it pay like it did before the goddamned war. Well, he kin always hope.'

'You aiming to vamoose and leave him to it?'

'I sure am. Seen too much slaving in my life. I aim to be a free man in a real way!'

Ross Clement, standing a little behind his father's shoulder, looked narrowly at Blick. He thought of the Navy pistol, which Joe still held. He thought abut Hal Coburn and the way he had looked at the gate that day when he had called to see Pete. He wondered about Hokay, suddenly turning up out of nowhere. An idea was beginning to form deep in his brain. In his mind's eye he saw – not Hokay – but Hal waiting out there among the trees or the rocks, with two guns instead of gold bars. It would not be a bullet in the back job as that was not Hal's style, but a challenge and a shoot-out, face to face and gun to gun. If that was the way it was, old Pete would come off worst because Hal was fast – too fast for the older man.

'I reckon,' he said quietly, some half-formed idea moving his lips, 'Hal Coburn is at Pierceville. That feller, Jesset, told me yesterday – when I was in town to look at the hotel – that Hal had said something about going today.'

It was a lie. He had not spoken to Jesset. Ross kept his voice composed as he spoke but his mouth was suddenly dry. Why had he said it? For a moment he was not sure but then he knew. It was a way out – for himself – and that was the most important thing in his life.

For a second his eyes met those of Blick. No hint of what was in Blick's mind could be seen but he knew his own mind had been read for a brief second although not fully understood.

'All right,' Pete was saying, 'have it your own way. I guess I can spare the time but if this turns out to be some wild-goose chase you won't see sundown, that's for sure.'

'I'll be seeing fifty dollars before sundown,' Blick answered, 'and then sundown will see me riding out of this territory!'

Pete told Ross to come with him and insisted on taking another couple of armed men along as a back-up as well as Ross: Bilt Cameron and the bearded man called Pepper. Shortly afterwards the little cavalcade set off from the outer gate with Blick leading on the saddle-less mare and wearing his shirt again but feeling naked and vulnerable without his gun.

He followed the trail as described by Hokay a few days before. He was quite unfamiliar with it but found that it presented no problems. Behind him, Pete Clement rode with a sour expression of suspicion. He was not too sure what to expect. There was a chance, he believed, that the gold really was awaiting him. If not he would make certain that Blick took a bullet in the back and his hand hovered near his side-gun at all times, ready for the first hint of treachery. He was keen also to set eyes on Hokay once again. Gold or no gold, he felt he wanted to settle with that low-down hobo for the worry and irritation of the past. A bullet would see to that. It would be a good riddance.

Pepper and Bilt had no real idea what they were out on the trail for except as guards to their employers but they accepted the situation and did not even think of asking any questions. The Clements were not the kind of men to welcome familiarity and never took anyone into their confidence. Pepper chewed tobacco and spat. Bilt went into a daydream about a girl he had known in Denver. Both felt that riding guard was better than a day's work on the ranch.

Of the party, Ross Clement was in the greatest turmoil of mind. The truth was – as he admitted fully for the first time – he hated his father who he believed had stood in his way throughout life. The idea that he could live fully only after his father's death had flickered somewhere in his subconscious for some years but until this morning it had never crystallized. Now he faced it and knew it to be true.

He had little conscience at the thought. As he saw it, his father was old and had had his day. Space must be made for Ross to fulfil his own dreams and these lay far afield in places his father had never visited and consisted of ambitions the older man had never thought of.

As Ross saw it, whatever happened today would be no fault of his. If he was right, and Hal Coburn lay in wait, then Pete's death would be the result of his own deeds in the past and Hal Coburn would have evened the score. Afterwards, Hal must die too. The rifles carried by Ross and his companions would see to that and it would all be perfectly justified in the eyes of the law. If he managed to turn tail and, by some fluke, make a getaway, then the lawmen must catch up with him. In either case Ross would be in the clear and all things would change for the better.

On the other hand, maybe this story about gold had some truth in it. If it did, then he meant to have all the loot. It was wealth that could be lifted and carried away and not deposited in the old man's bank account or tied up in stock.

He would have it. There was no doubt in his mind about that . . .

6

Hokay got up in the darkness of the night and set off with his mule cart along the familiar track. The mule had been well rested the day before and gave him no trouble. The gold bars were already on the cart and covered with sacking. He took all his spare clothes with him, which consisted of another pair of pants and an even older hat. He had no intentions of coming back. He reckoned it was now time for him to clear out of the territory.

It had not been such an easy decision to make. He had settled into his way of life as a forest-dweller pretty well and had not visualized making a change at any foreseeable time in the future, but the return of Hal had upset him. Also, the plan, which he himself had created, about getting rid of Clement once and for all had kept him in a worried state of mind ever since he had explained it to Blick.

The truth was he was scared of Pete Clement

and he realized that all sorts of things might go wrong. After the rancher was dead there would be a mighty shindig and an investigation, with men searching about like a lot of goddamned bloodhounds and no telling what they might come up with.

He was determined not to be around when that happened. The time had come to leave and start a new life somewhere else, well away from Sandstone.

At the time he had thought up the plan it had not worried him. It had seemed easy enough. He knew his marksmanship to be pretty good and he had, in fact, done a bit of bushwhacking before. Only once, certainly, when he had been a young feller in the trapping line and he had become aware of a guy following him through the wilderness, looking to steal his rifle and everything else he possessed. There were always polecats like that about. That one had paid for it with his life when Hokay let him have it from behind a lump of fallen timber. He had not killed anybody since but he had not lost his skill as his ability to survive in the woods testified.

In this case, he had an excellent place from which to do his bushwhacking and he had no compunction about ridding the world of a snake like Clement. Maybe his present nervousness was just the result of too many people seeming to be mixed up in it. There was Hal and Blick and Liza and the goddamned sheriff and guys from the ranch.

He could not be sure how many men Pete Clement might bring with him. He would be unlikely to come alone even if Blick seemed as friendly as could be but Hokay did not think there would be more than two bodyguards. Pete would not want many people to know about the gold – that was for sure. Anyhow, Hokay felt confident enough that he could settle about three when he caught them in the open. The first one, though, must be Pete Clement.

He knew that Hal had spoken to Somerville about the gold. It was what he had expected to happen when Hal and Blick had ridden away from the hogan that day, although he had not thought of it when he had been explaining things to them. Hal was bound to try to get his father's name cleared. Somerville, obviously, had not been convinced – particularly in the absence of the chief witness, Hokay, who had no intention of appearing in public view to be shot in the back some dark evening before he could get into the witness box. The other reason, of course, for the lack of action was Somerville's fear of Clement. He would not relish the task of telling Pete Clement to his face that he was suspected of robbery and murder. Somerville would much prefer to keep his head down about all of this and it was easy to dismiss Hokay as a half-crazy muskrat and hang on to the undoubted fact that the whole case had been settled years ago by Judge Elder.

This bushwhacking was certainly illegal and a crime in the eyes of the citizens of Sandstone but it seemed like justice just the same and would open the way for Hal and the girl to live a normal life.

That was the way Hokay saw it. He knew Blick felt much the same about the whole thing. It seemed to Hokay that he and Blick looked at the world from the same viewpoint, that is, from under the bushes, low down by the side of the trail.

Even so, having sorted it all out in his own mind, Hokay still felt nervous about it and wanted to get it over with.

It was still dark when the mule cart emerged from the cover of the forest track and crept towards the township. Deliberately, Hokay steered for the little house where Liza Hunter lived. He stopped a hundred yards from its vague outline and carried one of the gold bars to her garden gate. He left it just inside on top of her favourite clump of pansies. There was a note attached which he had scrawled out the evening before just before sundown.

Dear Miss Hunter,
  I'm leaving this hear gold bar with you because I

reckin you could do with it after all you've bin through. I'm taking the rest with me as I'm going to try to set up a new life someplace else. If you was to take the bar out to another township maybe you could get it changed for money. That's what I'll be doing although a guy like me will find it harder than you will because no-good fellers like me ain't trusted like regular schoolmarms and suchlike folks. Anyhow, the best of luck! I'll be using my bars as bait at first to catch a godd . . . a snake in the grass that should have been killed off years ago. Then I'll be hitting the trail like he . . . I'll be clearing off quick as lightning. Tell Hal it'll be all right now after the snake's been stamped on. The gopher is getting mad! Should have done this before but I didn't have the guts or the chance or the idea either. Look after yourself, Miss Hunter, and think kindly on Hal. He's a good young feller. One of the best!

So long

Hokay.

He crept silently back to his cart and set off once again through the early light. He took a round-about route to avoid the town and had gone some miles when a wheel went into a deep rut in the track. Cursing, he searched around for a length of wood to use as a lever and eventually found a branch that was just strong enough to do the job. He levered the wheel up to the edge of the hole and commanded his mule to move on so that the cart was soon back on solid ground. Even so the episode wasted a lot of time. He was held back further when the mule scented a bear and refused to budge. Very likely the bear had passed by hours before but the mule did not know that and resisted all attempts to move forward. Hokay was forced to take another way which wasted more time. When at last he reached the trees that signalled his near approach to his destination, the sun was well up.

Most of the area was well wooded but there was a clearing of stony, open hillside, then a flatter stretch, covered with small boulders, beyond which stood the large granite outcrop he had described to Blick.

In spite of the time already wasted on the journey, Hokay reckoned he had plenty of time and went unhurriedly about the business of preparing for the bushwhacking. First of all he stood the cart in front of the large granite rock. He wanted to make certain that when Clement showed up he would stop immediately in front of it. That would be just the right spot for Hokay to place a bullet from his hiding-place up on the slope. Then he released the mule from the traces, led her into the woods and tethered her safely under the trees. There was a chance that Clement might reach for a gun and the mule could get hit. That, to Hokay, seemed the worst thing that could happen.

That done, he clambered up the slope to the cleft in the rocks from which he intended firing his shot. It was a good vantage point, quite high up and well concealed. When he lay down flat in the stone trench he vanished from view and the hiding-place was made even better when he placed a number of boulders across it to create a short tunnel into which he could lie and drag himself backwards so that he was out of sight altogether even at a few feet of distance. Hokay called it his gopher-hole. He had thought about it often enough before and had always reckoned it would make a swell place for a bushwhacking if such a thing ever seemed necessary.

As he worked, he began to feel quite cheerful, his doubts of the night before vanishing in the morning light. He checked his rifle and placed it carefully at the edge of his hiding-place. He reckoned one bullet should do for Pete but there might be a couple of others so he fully loaded the gun just in case.

The next part of the plan he had in mind was to take the gold bars from the cart, hide them away for safety, and replace them with boulders under the sackcloth. It was then that things began to go wrong. He heard a horse snicker in the near distance and knew at once that he had no time to do anything further than run into his place of concealment.

He had scarcely settled himself, rifle at the ready, when Blick came out of the trees. Hokay saw him hesitate for a brief moment and then move forward at a trot, looking neither to right nor left as if he had not a care in the world. Then Pete Clement came into view, sitting up straight in the saddle, eyes widening as he caught sight of the cart with its heap of little boxes only half-covered by the sacking.

Some short distance behind and still out of sight under the trees rode Ross Clement with his two henchmen. Deliberately, he had hung back as he realized the direction in which Blick was leading them. His knowledge of the country told him they were approaching the open, rocky space and it occurred to him that this might be the spot where Hal would choose to make a fight of it. Then he caught sight of the wheel of the cart through a gap in the foliage and he knew he had guessed correctly that this was to be the place of action.

He held up a restraining hand to his two followers but uttered no word of warning. His father moved further ahead, quite unaware of the gap extending between himself and the others of the party and vanished round a slight bend in the trail.

Then came the boom of a rifle.

Out in the sunlight Pete Clement had been dazzled for a moment by the sudden change from the shade of the trees, but had looked up in surprise when he saw the cart. Before his mind fully registered the fact a fierce pain ripped through his body and he felt a sledge-hammer blow to the ribs. He did not hear the sound of the shot. The universe seemed to concentrate itself into the wild agony of the explosion within him. His horse moved from under him. He fell like a stone.

'Christ!' Pepper thrust his spurs into his mount and pushed past Ross and out into the light. He saw Pete Clement topple to the ground and some way ahead Blick setting his heels to the mare in an attempt to gallop from the scene. Pepper, gun already in hand, fired and Blick jerked wildly while his saddle-less horse leaped in sudden fear. Only with difficulty did the Negro hold on as the blood streamed from his wound and pain racked his body.

'What the hell, Mr Clement!' Bilt, moving past Ross on the narrow trail was looking amazed and fearful. 'We shouldn't ever have let the boss move out there alone!'

'Hold it!' Ross's command stopped him in his tracks. 'Move out there and you'll get it too. The old man's been bushwhacked! Hey, Pepper, git back! Take cover. We need to take care of that bastard. Find out where he's shooting from!'

He was right. Pepper understood and turned back under the trees. To run out into the open in an attempt to help Pete, even if he was still alive, would be to ask for another bullet. Better to do what Ross said but it seemed queer to Pepper that young Ross had hung back while his old man went ahead into that space and into danger.

His suspicions were correct although he did not fully realize the fact. In his heart Ross was pleased to see his father lying out there in the sunlight, body sprawling across the stones, one arm outstretched, and with no sign of life. It was as if a weight had been removed from his own soul.

However there was still the question of the gold. Ross knew it was there. He had seen the shape of the boxes under the sacking and recognized them for what they were. It was a surprise to him to learn that Blick had been telling the truth about the gold. He had expected no straightforward deal – only a shoot-out with Hal. The bushwhacking had come like a bolt from the blue. He did not believe that it came from Hal. It was not the feller's style. Some other polecat. Hokay! That was it! Smelly little Hokay!

So the bushwhacker had to be dealt with. There was no other way of getting the gold.

'Dismount, boys,' he whispered to his followers. 'We need to git up that slope behind him. That's where he's hiding out. We'll take him on three sides and blast his goddamned head to smithereens!'

Silently they moved to one side under the trees and began to spread out.

7

When Hal awoke at sunrise he looked around the farm for Blick and was surprised to see no sign of him At first he wondered if his friend was working in one of the outhouses even at that early hour, but there was no sound and no response to his call. Then he discovered that the mare had gone from the stable but without her saddle and he knew that Blick had crept out silently before dawn.

The idea amazed and hurt him because he had believed that a perfect trust existed between them. He went back into the house and pondered over the mystery as he poured coffee. There seemed no reason why Blick should creep off in the night and no obvious place he could have gone to.

Blick knew almost nobody in or around the town. There were only Hokay and Liza. There was the chance he had decided to ride back into the woods to speak with Hokay about something although that seemed very unlikely and there was no reason why he should creep away. Anyway it was a long ride through the dark and nobody would undertake it except out of dire necessity.

Could he have taken it into his head to visit Liza? There was no possible reason for it that Hal could think of but maybe he had wanted to talk to her. Certainly she had been kind to him. Perhaps there was something.

Hal placed his half-empty mug of coffee on the table and walked quickly from the building. Within minutes he had saddled his own horse and was riding through the morning light towards Liza's house. He realized soon enough that he himself wanted to see her. Not for any reason except that he liked to be in her company in spite of his recent resolution to leave her out of the dark tunnel of his own life.

When he came in sight of her little house he saw her in the garden, bending beside the gate. Her pony was already ready and waiting, newly saddled. She looked up as Hal called her name.

'Liza, have you seen Blick? He went missing this morning.'

'Oh, it's you, Hal!' she exclaimed. 'No, Blick hasn't been around here but I'm glad to see you. This thing . . . Look! It's a gold bar! Left by Hokay! There's a note too. I'm making for Somerville's office. This time he'll have to take notice.'

Hal was dumbfounded. He swung from the

saddle and gazed in amazement at the gold. Then he accepted the grubby note that she handed to him. He read it through, quickly to begin with, then a second time with much more care. He knew immediately what it meant. Hokay wasn't kidding about the bushwhacking. Somehow, Liza was thinking more of the gold bar and what effect it was likely to have on the sheriff. At the moment, Hal saw the planned killing as much more important. It came to him at the same time as he had the answer to the question of Blick's disappearance. Blick was mixed up in this too and had crept out in the night in order to prevent Hal attempting to stop him.

They were going to kill Clement and had invented a plan to bring the rancher to some quiet spot where he could be killed with a bullet fired from some place of hiding. That's where Hokay must come in. He was an expert shot and would have no hesitation in carrying out a plan that many men would regard as dishonourable. Hokay did not feel he could afford such principles. The world had always been against him and he did not think he owed it anything.

What about Blick? His part in it seemed clear enough also. Somebody had to take on the difficult task of leading the victim into the trap. Blick would do that if he believed he was really justified and Hokay's words in the note made the reason obvious enough. It seemed to be the only solution if Hal was ever going to have a normal life in Sandstone. Hokay was going to stamp on the snake and leave Hal in the clear. Blick would go along with that for the sake of his friend whatever the risks.

It was a dirty business, bushwhacking, but these two guys made it seem noble. Nevertheless, it was clear murder in the eyes of the law and it did not seem right to Hal that they should sacrifice whatever they had in life in the hope of making everything fine for himself – and Liza. The latter thought sprang into his mind in a sudden spark of emotion. These two ordinary fellers could see what was in his head maybe better than he could. Perhaps they could see something in Liza as well!

He pushed the idea out of his mind. It was too splendid a thought for this time. Maybe it would never be right. He stared hard at the dirty piece of paper, trying to draw a clue from it and as he did so one word seemed to spring from the page – gopher . . . *The gopher is getting mad!*

Hokay and old Billy had been friends for a long time. Hal remembered his father telling him something about Hokay and the gopher-hole. It was a place that seemed set up by nature for a bushwhacking. Billy had seen the spot and had laughed about it, knowing Hokay's earlier experience in that activity. He had pointed the place out to Hal when they had been out deer-hunting. Now only a vague recollection remained in Hal's mind. He had been only a boy at the time and the memory had dimmed.

Still, he had a fairly good idea where the place was. Perhaps he was right in thinking Hokay still saw it as the perfect spot . . .

'We need to see the sheriff, Hal.' Liza's voice penetrated his thoughts. 'This gold bar proves that Hokay was telling the truth about the gold and the rest of his story is likely to be accurate as well! Somerville has to take some action. He needs to investigate the whole thing again.'

'Well, in the absence of Hokay as an actual witness that might be doubtful,' objected Hal. 'He would have to be brought into it and the thing is, Liza, Hokay is heading right now into deep trouble. Don't you see what he means by the bushwhacking? He's out to get Clement and I'm sure Blick is in it too! They'll be on the wrong side of the law as much as Clement ever was. I'm going to do what I can to stop it. If anybody should be dealing with Clement it ought to be me!'

She stared at him. Always, she had known that he intended facing Clement in a gunfight at some time in the future, whatever the consequences to himself. She understood his way of thinking. In the absence of justice, revenge must take its place. It was the road to ruin but in the long term the knowledge that he had done nothing on behalf of his father would destroy him anyway.

'Let's bring in the law, Hal,' she pleaded. 'It's the only way that makes sense. Anyway, I'm heading into town right now to get Somerville out of his bed. If he does nothing I'll bring in the marshal from Silver City. That may be too late to help Hokay and Blick but it will put Somerville out of his job!'

She mounted her pony and he passed the heavy bar up to her, where it hung in her saddlebag. It would slow the pony down but it was necessary evidence required to waken up the sheriff and to focus his mind.

'All right, Liza. Tell Somerville that Clement is going to get shot and to make for the woods near Springwater. There's a big lump of granite there that most folks know about. Tell him to bring some men but not to go in shooting. Blick and Hokay ain't criminals yet and never will be in my mind!'

He turned his horse and galloped down the track and out of sight. Liza did not watch him go but turned her own pony towards the town. It seemed to take an age before she was in the main street and heading for the sheriff's office. There were a good many people up and about. The men doffed their hats to her and the few ladies called out a greeting. She responded to them all in spite of her troubled mind.

When she reached the sheriff's door, she found it closed but she thumped the iron knocker very hard and without ceasing until he made an appearance. He looked sleepy and irritated but opened his eyes wide in surprise when he saw her.

'This gold bar,' she said without preliminary, 'is part of the haul stolen from the Fletcher mine. As we said, Hokay has had it all this time. Also, you can see from this note that he intends killing somebody before he clears out of the country. Hal says that means Pete Clement is going to be bushwhacked. You're the sheriff, so do something to stop it. If you do nothing I'll bring in the marshal. So get some men together and we'll ride out to Springwater where that big granite rock is. There we'll find Hokay and maybe stop this happening. I mean it, Sheriff! I'll ride for the marshal today if need be!'

Somerville looked into her eyes and saw her determination. He read the note and knew he had to try to save Pete Clement. As sheriff it was his duty to try to do something about it. If he took a few men and was in time, it might work out. He did not relish the thought of falling foul of the marshal.

Also it seemed to him that a down-and-out like Hokay might not be too difficult to deal with. A strong posse ought to be able to bring him in, he hoped, before he could get started on his bushwhacking. To save the life of an important man like Pete Clement would be a feather in his own cap anyhow. Recovering the gold for the Fletcher mine was something else again. Maybe he could start making a name for himself at last, and if the marshal got to hear of his success, so much the better.

It was one of the few occasions when Somerville was galvanized into action. There was no time to waste and he set about gathering in the usual men as deputies plus a few others who were available. Within a short while they were mounted and ready to go, rifles and handguns at the ready. To his surprise, the young lady insisted upon riding with them. Liza was adamant in her determination in spite of the dangers which were pointed out to her. She did not state her reasons. She was not quite sure exactly what they were but knew she could not sit at home, waiting patiently for news.

At about the same time as Liza picked the gold bar from her garden that morning, the Reverend Phil Cranberry was climbing on to buckboard of his neat little buggy to sit beside his lady-friend, Winny. They were just about to set off from his small house at Magpie Drop. Tomorrow was the sabbath and it was necessary that he should get back to the church and manse at Sandstone in time to take the service in the morning. It was a considerable irritation as he much preferred staying at Magpie Drop, but duty called and he could not deny it.

Winny sat beside him, looking smart and comely enough – if a little plump – in her dark-blue outfit. She was explained to the outside world as his housekeeper and secretary but it was an open secret that she was more than that to him. Folks might disapprove but they had become accustomed to the situation and it was easier to pretend that the minister told the truth than that he was a liar.

That morning there was a pony hitched to the rear of the trap. Cranberry had found it a few days earlier standing outside his garden gate, looking lost and forlorn. It was a rough-looking beast of the kind used in cattle-work but the interesting thing about it was that it carried the brand of the Clement ranch. It seemed to have strayed a long way from home and the Reverend Cranberry intended returning it to Pete Clement, who was an important man and well worth currying favour with. The minister gave no thought to the possible fate of the pony's rider, at that moment lying in a shallow grave not far from Hokay's hogan, but assumed the animal had just wandered off on its own.

This errand meant a considerable detour from his usual route into Sandstone but he did not really mind when he thought of Clement's gratitude on getting the pony back. It was a fine morning and the minister was in a good humour. He attempted to keep Winny amused by telling her about the sermon he had prepared for the next day. He had included a joke regarding the Biblical quotation 'blessed are the peacemakers', comparing it to the new slang term for the Colt 45, 'the peacemaker', which he believed might have been used to good effect against the Philistines had it been around at the time. Winny laughed as she always did, without really feeling that there was anything funny about it.

For all the faults that people were inclined to see in them, they were not an unpleasant pair. They meant nobody any harm and often enough went out of their way to help others less fortunate than themselves. The Reverend Cranberry always spoke in a friendly way to Hokay when he saw him and once had given him the job of tidying up the manse garden. He had paid him well enough too, using church funds, of course, which was only right. He had not seen Hokay for some time but gave that no thought.

Late in the forenoon, the Reverend Cranberry and his lady were following a track through timber when they heard shots from somewhere in the distance.

'Hunters,' said the Reverend Cranberry confidently.

'Yes,' agreed Winny. 'Queer, isn't it, that people always have to be killing.'

It was the truest and wisest remark she had made for some time, and - unfortunately – it was the last remark of its kind she ever made.

When Hal left Liza he rode as fast as his mount would take him to the north-west. He travelled for a good many miles, gradually moving into the area of scattered trees he remembered so well from earlier years. He heard the same shots as had Cranberry, but from a longer distance. He slowed down, not wishing to ride straight into trouble. There was a thick patch of forest just ahead, which he approached with great caution but entered it without sensing danger.

The narrow track soon petered out and he was forced to dismount and lead the roan slowly. For a time he felt himself to be losing his way but then he came to a clearing by a small stream and a memory came back to him from the days of his boyhood when he had hunted deer there with his father.

He knew the granite slab was not far ahead. That was where Hokay had his gopher-hole. It was there that he was planning to carry out this crazy bushwhacking which would make criminals out of himself and Blick. Shots had already been fired. Probably it was too late.

His heart sank at the thought. If Clement had been killed it meant that he himself was relieved of the need to avenge his father, but the price paid by Hokay and Blick was too high. The thought of Blick was uppermost in his mind. Blick had been badly dealt with in the world and only now did it seem that he might make something out of his life. Now he was about to throw away the chance out of a sense of loyalty to his friend.

Hal stopped for a moment as a sense of despair ran through him, then he pushed on through the trees, rifle at the ready.

8

Ross Clement was bent double as he clambered up the slope of boulders and loose scree. He had worked his way around so that he now believed he was in the rear of the bushwhacker. Over to his right, Pepper was doing the same, grey hair just showing amid the rocks. Bilt was somewhere to the right, out of sight for the moment. All eyes were narrowed to catch a glimpse of the assassin. At every movement they stopped to listen, desperate to find Hokay before he caught sight of one of them and fired another accurate bullet.

Hokay lay still in the gopher-hole, eyes just on a level with a slab of shale that he knew fitted over the small open space now occupied by his head. His body was entirely concealed in the narrow six-foot tunnel overlaid by other pieces of stone. If he had drawn himself backwards and edged the shale slab into place he would have vanished like a snail into its shell. That, in fact, had been his plan. He

111

had reckoned on shooting Clement and then disappearing while the rancher's companions searched in vain for some sign of the exact spot from which the shot had been fired, to emerge later when the coast was clear. Then he had planned to get his gold and make his getaway with Blick as his fellow-conspirator, good friend and future companion in a life of leisure.

Now, though, Hokay's nerves were on edge. He had become aware of the approach of Clement and his men before he had had time to hide the gold and replace it with the empty boxes. He had been further unnerved when he saw Blick being hit and ride away wounded into the woods. He needed to get out of the hole to help Blick if possible but there were enemies nearby and to show himself would be likely to be fatal.

He did not know how many men Clement had brought with him because they had not come into view but had hung back in the woods while their boss rode out into the open. That was a queer thing in itself. Most guys would have been keeping a look-out in a situation like this just in case of trouble. Hokay thought there could not be more than two or three others. There had been little noise, for one thing, and he did not believe that Clement would have wanted many of his men to know about the gold. He would want it for himself and the law could not be allowed to hear of it.

Away over near the trees Blick's saddle-less horse stood quiet, having recovered from its fright. Blick himself must be over there somewhere, hiding and nursing his wound, or perhaps already dead. The idea jumped around in Hokay's brain like a jack-rabbit. He bit his lip, uncertain of his next move.

Half-way down the rocky slope, Bilt Cameron shifted his position. There was a large boulder a little higher up. If he could shield his body behind it he would be protected while he sought a better view of Hokay's position. He pushed himself forward and for a second his shoulder was raised. Hokay from above spotted the sudden flash of blue and his agitation caused him to pull the trigger of his rifle. Even as he fired he knew he had made a mistake, for he had given away his position. He heard Bilt yelp in sudden agony as the bullet ripped across his shoulder, sending blood in a sudden stream down into his shirt.

Ross Clement and Pepper heard the shot and saw the puff of smoke at the same time. Ross bounded up through the rocks and within seconds was standing over Hokay's hideout. Hokay had not time to hide his head or to regret his hasty action. Ross already had drawn his side-gun and pulled the trigger. The bullet, fired at close range, opened up the back of Hokay's skull. Almost at the same second, Pepper scrambled up beside Ross and his rifle bullet thundered into the same part of Hokay's head.

Blood and bone broke through the lank hair. A great goblet of red welled up and overflowed. Hokay jerked once and his face slumped into the earth, only the back of his shattered head visible in the entrance to his little tunnel.

Ross and Pepper stared – then Ross kicked earth and pebbles into the gaping wound.

'Goddamned reptile,' he snarled. 'Lie and rot where you are!'

'Yeah,' agreed Pepper. 'Low polecat killed the boss like as if it was nothing.'

Pepper started off down the slope, anxious about Bilt and was relieved to discover that the shoulder wound was only a graze.

'Let's go see the boss,' he said. 'Who would have thought of him getting killed like that!'

'I'll go see the old man!' Ross yelled out with a trace of irritation in his voice but with no hint of sorrow. 'You two collect in that gold. Bring in that black man's horse and load it up. Use Pete's horse as well if you need to but get the gold!'

Bilt and Pepper stared in astonishment. Ross Clement seemed more concerned about the gold than about the death of his father. They watched as he walked quickly down the slope and crossed the open space towards his father's supine form. He stood stock-still but did not remove his hat from his head.

Ross Clement realized with a sudden shock that his father was not yet dead. Blood was still pumping from the old man's body indicating that the heart had not quite given up.

For a moment, Ross tensed. He felt as if the ground was moving beneath his feet and was threatening to engulf him. Even now, his father, lying helpless in the dirt, seemed to loom over him as he had done throughout life. The old eyes opened slightly and seemed to hold a flicker of recognition as they focused upon the younger man. The lips parted a little as if to speak but there came no sound. Ross tightened his mouth and his hand hovered briefly above his side-gun. Then he turned away. He knew his father could not last long. That much was evident.

Pepper and Bilt had taken in the saddle-less mare and were leading it towards the cart. Bilt was looking at the ground as he walked as if deep in thought. The drying blood showed on his shirt but he did not seem badly hurt. Pepper's eyes were on Ross. Even at the distance of about fifty yards he looked puzzled.

Ross began to walk quickly towards them, knowing, without really thinking about it, that he feared they would discover that Pete still lived.

'Check the gold!' he ordered. 'How much is on that cart?'

It did not matter how much was there as long as

it was a sizeable amount and none of it was lying about amid the rocks. He gave the order and asked the question to divert their eyes from his father. Ross recognized his own purpose even as he spoke. He did not want them to know that his father still lived.

He reached the cart and held up a hand as if to prevent them going any further. They stopped and watched as he drew back the sacking from the boxes and opened them to the light. All gasped as they caught the gleam of gold.

'Jeeze,' whispered Pepper, 'that's a goddamned fortune!'

Ross's eyes were wide and seemed to glow in the reflected light of the precious metal. For a second he forgot his two companions. It was as if a golden door had opened for him to enter into palace of great splendour. So the black man had been telling the truth about the gold, only he had forgotten to mention the price to be paid. . . .

'What about Mr Clement?' Bilt was asking. 'That shot just killed him straight off, I guess.'

It was a guess that sounded almost like a question. Ross tightened his mouth.

'There ain't nothing to be done about that,' he growled. 'Just get this here stuff on to the horses. We're taking it with us and quick! No time to waste!'

The two men looked into his face and saw his

mood. Ross Clement was in a fiery state of mind. It was evident that he was rapidly reaching a point where anger could take over and he would reach almost instinctively for his guns They carried out his orders and loaded the mare with gold-filled boxes wrapped in the old sacking. Two of the boxes lost their rotten lids as they lifted them but they hung quite safely. Ross led his father's horse over also but there was no need to use it as a pack-horse. The mare seemed able to carry the gold bundles well enough.

Bilt looked over at the prone form His voice took on a nervous edge as he ventured to speak.

'What about Mr Clement? We'll need to take him back with us. We could lift him across the saddle of his horse—'

'That ain't the way I want my father carried,' snapped Ross. 'We'll send people later.'

'Yeah, but the thing is, Mr Clement, there's animals prowling around – coyotes and such. It don't seem right. Might be better—'

'Forget it!' snapped Ross in a tone that seemed to brook no argument. 'We can send somebody pretty soon. Let's move out of here. This way – it's easier riding.'

He led them by a track that led away from the open space towards the trees and avoided going near Pete Clement. Whether it was better riding was questionable and their minds jumped as they suspected some other reason for the manoeuvre.

Nevertheless, there was no argument as they took a trail that seemed to lead westwards. As they rode, Pepper kept looking from side to side.

'Wonder where that black feller got to?' he asked at last. 'He's carrying my slug, sure as hell.'

'Dead in the woods,' replied Ross laconically.

Nothing further was said for some time as they made their way through the woodlands. The track was narrow and they rode in single file. At length it became clear to Bilt that it was leading in the wrong direction for the town or even for the ranch.

'This here gold will be a welcome sight to the sheriff,' he remarked almost as if in easy conversation, although his mind buzzed like a swarm of hornets. 'This is surely the Fletcher mine stuff. Could be a big reward coming!'

'Yeah,' said Ross drily.

A little way ahead the trail opened out into a little clearing. Ross remained silent until they got to it and then held up his hand to signal a halt. He turned to face them, his features empty of expression.

'Time we got a couple of things straight, fellers. This is the Fletcher gold, sure enough, but these mining bosses have long since given up looking for it. If they offer a reward it won't be a tenth of what the stuff's worth because they're all as mean as hell and don't believe in playing fair with anybody. As for the sheriff, we ain't in the business of making things better for him. Somerville's always been a lousy sheriff, as you know, so nobody owes him any favours.

'What we're going to do is stash this gold in a secure place and keep it for ourselves.' He stopped speaking for a moment to study their expressions of astonishment and doubt before continuing: 'There ain't no use taking it back to the ranch because there are too many guys up there with big eyes and bigger mouths. We hide it in a place I know and then share it between the three of us. One third of this gold to each and we'll be rich men. I know you two fellers have done nothing but work your guts out all your lives but now is the chance to make it all different. What do you say?'

Ross believed they would agree to the plan. The gold was as great a temptation to Pepper and Bilt as it was to himself. If through weakness or conscience or fear they did not agree then he must shoot them now instead of later.

There came no immediate answer from either of the two ranch-hands. Pepper stared at the ground. Bilt glanced back along the trail as if he was still thinking about Pete. Ross moved his horse forward a step and drew the sacking back from one of the gold bars on the mare's back. It gleamed in a ray of sunlight penetrating the surrounding branches. The movement caused his companions to stare at the gold bar. Ross saw greed and the lust for gold come into their eyes.

'All right,' he decided. 'Let's get going!'

Ross led the way with increased confidence along the narrow forest track. He knew where he was going. There was a place a long way from the ranch and the township and from any homestead, where the gold could be made safe until he had made contact with a certain dealer in the gold business who would take it off his hands at a good price with no questions asked. He had no genuine plan for sharing with Pepper and Bilt. They could vanish in the wilderness. Sometimes it happened that way – cowhands became tired of working for the same boss and wandered elsewhere. Usually nobody asked many questions.

He whistled a little tune to himself as his spirits rose. Pepper and Bilt heard it and were struck anew by his indifference to his father's death. Both wondered about old Pete and why it was they had not been permitted to get near the body. They also guessed at the answer.

Nevertheless, they made no further comment. There was the promise of riches ahead and the certainty of a gunfight if they pushed Ross too far. Neither of them cared very much for old Pete anyway and the sight of the gold drew them on their way like salmon bait in an otter trap.

Not long after renewing their journey the trail hit another wider path. Ross recognized it as one of the routes leading eventually to the Clement ranch, which lay some miles to the east. He turned in the other direction. He knew of another track further on which would help him on his way.

Suddenly there came a crash as some of the old sacking gave way and three gold bars fell from the mare's back to the ground.

'Damn!' shouted Ross, then he waited with as much patience as he could muster for Bilt and Pepper to dismount in order to retrieve it.

Just then there came the sound of hoofs and the swish of wheels as a pony and trap came round a bend only a few yards away. There was a man and a woman on the buckboard and a spare pony brought up the rear. It came to a slow halt. The man and woman both stared in surprise at the unexpected meeting.

Ross recognized them. It was the Reverend Phil Cranberry and the woman called Winny, whom he liked to pass off as his housekeeper. Ross felt his anger rising. His nostrils widened slightly and his fingers opened instinctively over his side-guns.

'Well, well, Mr Clement, isn't it?' The face behind the dog-collar broke into a smile. 'We are just on our way to see you or your father. Didn't expect . . .'

His voice trailed off as he saw the gold lying in

the dirt. Puzzlement came into his eyes.

'Hey, that's gold, isn't it?' blurted out Winny incautiously.

Ross knew they had seen too much. It seemed to him to be a certainty that he could afford to leave no witnesses. It was a stroke of very bad luck but he solved it in the way he generally solved every problem.

The sound of the two shots from his Colt .44 rang out into the trees all around. The Reverend Cranberry jerked violently as blood gushed from his mouth and in a second he had crashed from the buckboard to the ground. The pony swerved to one side in fright but Winny remained where she was, leaning back with a bloody bullet hole in the centre of her forehead. Her parasol fell from her fingers to the dirt.

Bilt and Pepper, in the act of picking up gold bars, stared in horror. Bilt let his load slip from his hands.

'Jesus Christ!' he groaned. He straightened up to stare at Ross, a drop of blood falling from the graze in his shoulder.

For a moment or two there was silence but for the restless movement of the horses. The minister lay with no further twitch or movement. Winny looked like a woman in a fainting-fit except for the mess of blood on her forehead.

'There was nothing else for it.' Ross sounded a

little defensive as if he had been forced to shoot a mad dog. He swung round in the saddle and looked closely at his followers. 'There ain't no use troubling yourselves too much about this. It had to be done and that's the finish of it. We're all in this together. Keep that in mind.'

His eyes had turned cold. They held the expression of a gunman ready to deal out death. The fact that he had just killed two people brought no guilt. It had been an inconvenience which threatened to make matters more difficult, but that was all. He was ready to do the same thing again if it seemed necessary.

Bilt and Pepper recognized his frame of mind. He was in the saddle with his guns under his hovering fingers. One Colt, they knew, was still hot and itched to be used again. They made no answer but went on loading the mare.

'You guys will get your share and you'll be glad of it!' went on Ross, his tone changing to one of good humour. 'You'll be rich! Your whole life will change. I know just the place to hide all this stuff until we can share it between us. All we have to do is keep our mouths shut until that day arrives. Hurry it up though, fellers, this trail is used too often to suit me.'

Soon afterwards they were again on their way, leaving the grisly scene behind them. Bilt and Pepper were hard men in themselves, but the murder of two innocent people struck them to the heart. Nevertheless, they felt themselves to be well and truly committed to the course of action Ross had drawn up for them. It seemed also that if Ross's plans fell through then the gallows would overshadow them all.

A mile or so further on and they cut away from the main trail to take another narrow track. It was fairly steep and they could not push the horses on too quickly. Ross knew it and he remembered too the stretch of old storm-felled timber lying up ahead. In his mind he saw almost exactly where the gold could be well hidden and the brushwood in which two corpses could lie for years without discovery.

9

Hal led his horse with caution under the low branches as he neared the open space where he believed Hokay had planned the shooting. He had heard shots from some distance away but he was too old a campaigner to ride recklessly into an unknown situation. In any case the terrain leading from the east did not allow for very rapid movement.

He came out of the forest at the steep base of the slope and there he left his mount, while he climbed slowly and as silently as possible towards the crest of the rocky little hill. He remembered fairly well where the gopher-hole was situated – well up the opposite slope from which it commanded a good view of the flat stretch of boulder-strewn ground beyond.

Hal carried his rifle in his hand and his Colt hung by his side. All seemed quiet but that could be a sign of danger, as he well knew.

Soon he raised his head carefully over the boulders on the summit of the hill and peered at the scene below. The huge granite rock was in plain view and before it stood the mule cart, empty and abandoned. There was no sign of the mule or of Hokay. There was a horse, saddled and bridled, standing patiently near the trees. Not far from the horse there lay the still figure of a man. Hal narrowed his eyes and looked for a long moment. There was no sign of movement and he concluded very quickly that he was looking at a corpse. It lay on its back but with the shoulders twisted almost as if the man had attempted to rise before death came to him.

The distance was too far to make out more except that he wore grey clothing and still carried a gun in his belt. The hair of the man was also grey. Hal bit his lip with a strange mixture of feelings. It looked to him as if Hokay had been successful.

Slowly he eased himself forward amid the stones and inched his way to where he thought he would find the gopher-hole. He came across it more quickly than he had expected. Still bent double in an effort to keep out of sight, he looked down at Hokay's shattered head and blood-soaked shoulders, still half-concealing the barrel of that old but deadly rifle.

For a moment or two Hal did not move. He was not shocked for he had seen too much of death to be much disturbed at the sight of blood and bone. Instead he felt a profound sadness and a terrible bitterness as he realized that he had arrived too late.

At the same time he was acutely aware of danger. The body of Pete Clement still lay over there in the open. It seemed to imply that the men who had killed Hokay could not be far away as they must surely intend to take the rancher home. Hal could well understand why they had shot the bushwhacker. It had been done out of revenge and self-defence. Anybody would have done the same. Rage and fear would demand such action.

He could not tell exactly who these men were. He guessed that Pete Clement would have been accompanied by one or two of his ranch-hands or even by his son before he ventured to be led to the gold. The old man had not been a fool – at least not as far as Hal knew. It came as a sudden jump of surprise in his mind to find he was thinking of Pete as an *old* man, but it did not lessen the terrible sense of injustice he carried on behalf of his father. Anyway, the man was now dead and that should be an end to it, but not in the way Hal had ever visualized.

He could not understand why there was no sound or trace of the men who had killed Hokay. They would not have ridden back to the ranch or even to find the sheriff and left Pete lying there.

He arose slowly to his feet, acutely aware of the possibility that he was being observed from the forest but determined also to give no sign that he was implicated in the shooting.

There was a chance, of course, that they might simply assume that his known feud with Pete Clement over the death of his father meant that he was likely to be behind the shooting, but that could only be by men who did not know him well. He had never been a bullet-in-the-back fighter.

He came down the slope, rifle at the ready, and walked slowly over to Pete Clement. As he approached he became more and more certain that he was not being observed. It would have been all too easy to have challenged him in the sight of a rifle or to have opened fire if that had been in their minds.

When he reached the still form, Hal stopped, his mind a curious mixture of emotion. This man had killed his father in cold blood and had brought about the death of his mother. The thought brought an upsurge of anger as it always did but now it was muted by the sight of the pathetic figure before him. The grey jacket was ruffled and bloodstained, the legs twisted as if in the pain of death. One arm was outstretched as if in appeal, the face, half hidden by a broad-brimmed hat, showed only a mouth curled in agony and shock.

Not for the first time, Hal realized the impossibility of anger against a dead man . . . at least one who lay as a corpse at his feet.

Then he saw the rim of the hat move slightly and the eyes came into view, dim but open, almost blind but not dead. The head turned slowly and the lips moved as if attempting to speak.

Hal stared and then bent over the grey figure as if to bring aid to the dying man. That Pete Clement *was* dying was evident. There was too much blood for it to be otherwise. But he had been deserted too, and by the men who had taken revenge on Hokay.

'You hearing me, Clement?' he asked. He spoke loudly, feeling the need to penetrate the fog of death. 'Can you speak?'

The dim eyes focused and slowly brightened a little as recognition came.

'Jesus!' The voice was no more than a hoarse whisper. 'You're Hal Coburn . . . You here to finish me off . . . ?'

'Not that . . . . It's over with. Hokay saw to that by the look of it. Where's your men? They ride off some place?'

Clement drew in a sharp breath then he spat blood into the dirt.

'Yeah, they did. They took . . . the gold. I saw . . . them do that . . . my son too. My blessed son! He knew it . . . knew I was still . . . could see I . . . still lived . . . but the gold mattered more to him . . . than I did. Might have guessed it was his way. I'm dying. I kin feel that. He knew it too! But he took the gold and left me to die.' He spat more blood over his chin and neck. 'Might have known . . .'

His body jerked violently and his face twisted anew in pain.

'They get that bastard . . . the one who did . . . the shooting?' he asked through his blood-filled mouth. 'They get him?'

'Yeah, they got Hokay. You see a black feller mixed up in this?'

'Goddamned liar lead me into it. They shot him. Serves him right too.'

'What happened to him? Did you see?'

'Nope. He was on a mare . . . no saddle. Hope the bastard's dead like I soon will be. What did they do it for, eh, you know? Somethin' to do with old Billy . . . was it?'

'Yeah, but I wasn't mixed up in this even though you killed my father. You did that just because you wanted the gold and because you killed Becky Hunter – that kid! You remember these things?'

'I remember all right. Always have done. God, I have always been sorry about the kid! But that was . . . an accident. Your pa was different. That was for the gold. Just like now. I wanted the gold. Now Ross wants the gold. Damn the gold . . . .'

Hal curbed the feeling of renewed anger that

130

arose in his heart at the bluntness of the admission that Pete's bullet had silenced old Billy just to keep the secret of the gold. Pity for the dying man went out of him. Then he thought of Blick. The thought of his friend being somewhere around in the woods with a bullet in him made Hal straighten up.

'I can't do anything much for you, Clement,' he said, with little regret. 'I would if there was any way but there ain't. I'm going to look for my friend – the black feller who you say is carrying a bullet. Hang on as best you can. I think there will be people here soon.'

'Yeah but I won't be. Go look for your buddy. You don't owe me nothin' that's for sure. . . .'

Hal searched around the hard open ground without finding anything of note. Then he went back to retrieve his horse and rode out past the granite rock to an area of rough grass bordering the woods. Here he saw tracks made by the passage of horses though they soon petered out as the track hit stony ground.

He sat in the saddle and looked around the grass and shrubs leading into the woods. There was no sign of Blick. A wounded man feeling himself likely to be pursued by his enemies would be looking for cover. After a moment's thought Hal urged his mount forward and rode over the grassy area to the trees, where he went along the margin of the wood and peered into the shadows as best he could.

He called out Blick's name a few times without result and then dismounted and searched closely every dark clump of undergrowth that he could see, where a wounded man might lie. He led the roan for some distance until he reached a place where the grass came to an end. Here the dirt track again came into view and he saw more hoof-marks. There was one that he recognized. It was odd because the shoe did not match its partners on the other hoofs of the animal. Blick had fitted that shoe on the mare about a couple of weeks previously. They had still been on the trail then and it was all they had with them. He had never got around to renewing it.

If the mare was being led away might not Blick still be mounted on it but as a prisoner? It was a possibility There was no sign of him here. Hal mounted and rode with increasing speed along the track in the same direction as had been taken by the little cavalcade before him.

In the depths of the woods Blick stirred in his hiding-place behind a fallen tree. He had been lying there for a long time, biting his lips to prevent himself from crying out from the pain of his wound. He knew the bullet was lodged in the muscles of his back but had dared not make a sound for fear he might be heard.

He had listened to Ross and his two men talking as they went by. Their voices were faint because they were some distance away, but he had come to believe that they had gone past the part of the forest which hid him. He had tried to get up then but sudden faintness overcame him and he fell into unconsciousness.

When he came to it was to hear his name being called from what seemed to him to be a great distance. He felt convinced Hal was there and forced himself to stand. He attempted to answer but no sound came from his dry lip. He then staggered through the undergrowth until he came to a spot where the trees seemed to thin out. There he saw Hal on the roan riding away at increasing speed up the forest track.

How far Hal rode before he heard gunfire he did not know. There were two or three shots at some distance and his heart sank as he imagined Blick falling with a fatal wound. Anything might have happened: Blick could have attempted to escape or perhaps they had just decided to kill him in a fit of anger or irritation as their minds seethed with the desire for revenge.

He followed the same track for some time until he judged it prudent to leave it and make his way through the woods in expectation of finding the main trail further on. He knew the dangers of following too closely on the heels of dangerous men and his sense of direction had sharpened with his years spent in wild country during the war.

When he came to the main trail, which he knew led eventually to the Clement ranch, he recognized it immediately although he had not seen it for a long time. He rode along its edge with the thin twigs of the trees brushing his shoulders. At every moment he expected to see Ross and his companions or to find the body of Blick lying in the dirt.

He drew in his breath with shock when he came across the buggy, pulled into the rough grass of the other side, almost under the branches, with the two ponies grazing quietly and the two corpses looking like a portrayal of death.

Hal recognized the Reverend Cranberry even as he lay face down with his fingers seeming to claw into the earth. Hal remembered him as a somewhat ineffectual man of the cloth, tedious in his sermonizing but quite harmless. He did not know the woman who leaned back on the buckboard with her forehead a mass of blood.

He saw it for what it was: cold blooded murder, for there could be no reason for killing such people except viciousness or a perceived need to silence them because they had seen too much.

That, of course, must be the reason for it. They had seen the gold and could not be allowed to live long enough to tell of it. It meant that Ross

Clement had no intention of returning the gold to its real owners. He meant to keep it to himself and his followers, which was the reason too for deserting his dying father.

Anger rose in Hal as he gazed at the murder victims. He became convinced also that Blick had been dealt with in the same way but that his corpse lay hidden somewhere in the woods near the granite rock. He put his hand on his rifle, remembering how he had loaded it before setting out. He checked his handgun also, feeling sure both weapons would soon be needed.

The idea of waiting for the sheriff to arrive with a posse did not occur to him. He had no faith in Somerville. Many hours could pass before Sandstone law made an appearance even if it came at all. Hal did not even consider waiting or riding back for help. Every instinct told him there was no time to waste if these murderers were to be caught up with.

He found tracks in the grass about a mile further on. They led towards the north. As far as he could make out there were four horses. One, he felt sure, carried the gold. That would be Blick's mare, the one animal without a saddle, and now without a rider.

He followed the tracks with care but they petered out when the grass gave way again to hard ground. Even so, he continued in the same direction as there seemed no reason why the men should have changed their route, and was rewarded when he saw, here and there, a faint print or a stone dislodged by a passing hoof.

Gradually, the terrain changed to a long rising gradient consisting mostly of long, coarse grass interspersed by outcrops of rock. The trees he had ridden through were now behind him but far off on the horizon he could see more forest, high timber, with ragged gaps against the sky where felling had taken place.

For many hours he saw no sign of his quarry apart from the trail through the grass, but at length, in the late afternoon, he caught a glimpse of a rider who appeared briefly from behind a huge boulder only to vanish again.

Hal hesitated, drawing the roan to a halt. He had no wish to be seen until he had approached closely enough to get to grips with Ross and his men. He was determined to settle with them. The memory of the slaughtered people on the road and the knowledge that Blick lay dead somewhere out in the woods put all other thoughts out of his mind.

There was, however, no adequate cover, and there was no prospect either of searching out some other route by which he could get near to them without being seen. There was nothing for it but to go on, keeping as low a profile as he could behind the stands of rock as he came to them.

Far ahead, Ross Clement turned in the saddle and peered back with narrowed eyes over the long way he and his companions had ridden. Some short distance ahead, Pepper and Bilt came to a halt also and squinted round at him, wondering at the short delay. Ross had been insistent upon wasting no time and had allowed no rest throughout their journey, regardless of the needs of the horses.

'Goddamn!' Ross cursed as he caught sight of the upper part of Hal's body as he climbed slowly up the incline in the distance. 'Here's thet damned soldier boy right on our trail . . .'

'Come again?' yelped Bilt. 'Who did ya say?'

'Hal Coburn. Large as life. Here he comes looking for trouble – and he'll get it!'

'Jeeze,' said Pepper. 'Reckon he knows about the gold?'

'And the rest!' snapped Bilt. The murder of Cranberry rankled with him. It had seemed a bit too much – even to keep the secret of the gold.

Ross recognized the tone. He did not react. His plans for silencing Bilt and Pepper were still very much in his mind. Right now, though, he still needed them both.

'Thet Coburn guy, he's the one who set up the bushwhacking,' he stated with conviction. 'He's the one who's been carrying the grudge about his old man being killed and been blaming my father with it! There ain't no doubt that he set up Hokay to do the dirty work. Now he's out to get us too – and the gold!'

'Yeah, could be that's the way it is,' answered Pepper. 'It was his black man who led us into it! How can he have the nerve to follow us up like this?'

'Nobody else with him by the looks of things,' grunted Bilt. 'He sure has guts, I'll give him that!'

'Sure,' Ross twisted his face into a snarl, 'but it ain't going to do him no good now. Time we settled with him. All right, move the horses over aways down the slope and then dismount and take cover. We'll show him bushwhacking – three times over!'

10

Ross and his two followers dismounted and Pepper led the four horses further on for about a hundred yards to a place where the ground evened out but was well out of sight of Hal Coburn at his present distance. There was an old shack with its roof half-off and a saw-pit which had been used by the timber men in time gone by. Pepper led the horses round the back of the shack and left them tethered to an old piece if fencing. He slapped the mare on the rump as if to remind her to look after her precious burden, then he ran up the slope to take cover behind a boulder.

Ross had selected his position about twenty yards away using an outcrop of granite. He lay along its top surface, shoulders and body well concealed by a chunk of rock that rose unevenly towards the sky. Further over to the left and a little ahead of Ross, Bilt lay flat on the ground, peering through a clump of brushwood.

The sun was beginning its swift slide to the western horizon. Soon the short dusk of those latitudes would be upon them. Still it was possible to see a fair distance down the long hillside. It would be a matter of getting this business done quickly before the light of day gave out but there was a danger too in trying to hurry things along.

'Wait for him to git real close,' called Ross in a voice loud enough for his companions to hear but too low to reach the ears of their enemy. 'When I give the signal, blast him to hell!'

Hal took a long time to get within rifle range. He realized he had lost sight of the horsemen up ahead and was aware of the possibility that he had been seen. As he came on he took care to continue to take as much cover as he could from the rock outcrops. He did not consider dismounting. If Ross was still riding out of sight behind the crest of the hill he would soon pull well ahead of a man on foot.

It was Bilt who fired the first shot. He saw the upper part of Hal's body appear just above a little hillock. Even in the dimming light, it made quite a good target although barely within range of a rifle bullet. To be certain of striking his quarry Bilt ought to have waited some more minutes but he did not do so. He was not sure within himself why he chose to fire so soon.

It was something to do with the whole set-up;

leaving old Mr Clement, the suspicion that the old man might still be alive, the deaths of the Reverend Cranberry and his woman, and now this bushwhacking without really knowing what Hal might have had to do with Hokay's action. It all seemed wrong somehow. Added to all of that, the pain from the broken, bleeding skin made by Hokay's final bullet was interfering with his train of thought. But he did not consciously shoot to miss. It was just that something in his mind told him to pull the trigger when he had little chance of hitting the target.

So he fired and the bullet went over Hal's head with six feet to spare. Hal swung the roan and plunged out of sight. In a moment he was on the ground, rifle at the ready.

Ross cursed and glared at the back of Bilt's head as it showed through the brushwood. He did not believe that the early shot had been an accident or a genuine misjudgement. Bilt was much more reliable than that when he wanted to be.

'Good to know who your friends are,' thought Ross, forgetting – for the moment – that friendship needs to go both ways.

Hal crouched amid the stones, striving to catch a glimpse of the enemy who had fired on him but there was nothing to be seen from his position. He hesitated only a moment and then began to crawl out to the right, slithering from rock to rock and gradually working his way up the long slope. At length, he saw a tiny, metallic glint near the top of a granite slab. He guessed it was a spur on the heel of a man who lay patiently in wait in the dead silence, not quite as well concealed as he had thought himself to be.

Hal considered whether to fire. At best he could inflict only a leg wound but it might well be enough to put one of his adversaries out of action. At the same time his own position would once again be made clear and he could expect a fusillade of shots in return.

The decision was taken out of his hands as a bullet came from somewhere up the slope to his right, ripped across the back of his jacket and opened the skin of his back in a long graze. He felt the blood gush down the inside of his shirt. He bit his lip but gave an involuntary groan of pain. In the silence that followed the crack of the rifle he could be clearly heard even from some distance away.

'By Christ!' Pepper's yell of triumph pealed through the air from a clump of rocks on the slope overhead. 'He took thet one, I reckon!'

Hal made no more sound but rolled to one side until he believed he was once more under cover Inwardly, he cursed himself for his momentary lapse of observation but then crawled with all the speed he could muster to another spot further over amid the long grass where another boulder offered protection.

Then he heard Ross Clement call out from his granite hiding-place, asking Pepper whether he was certain of his success.

'Sure of it! Goddamned well sure of it!' came the answer. 'You heard him!'

'Finish him off then,' came the order. Ross's voice sounded somehow detached and cold as if he himself was not mixed up in the affray 'Hey, Bilt, goddamned polecat's been hit bad. Git down there and finish him off!'

Hal, peering through the grass, made out the figure of Bilt as he rose to his feet. He thrust forward his rifle barrel and took swift aim. Bilt made an easy enough target as he stood against the comparative brightness of the sky. Hal tightened his finger on the trigger but did not fire. There was something guileless about Bilt's posture as he stood there, seeming for the moment uncertain as to what to do. More than that, the tone of Ross Clement's voice seemed to hold another idea that was not expressed. . . .

Then came the boom of a third rifle and Bilt pitched face down.

'Jeeze, was that . . . ?' came Pepper's strained voice, full of anxiety and disbelief.

'Yeah, stinking rat had another shot left in him!' yelled Ross.

Pepper did not doubt Ross's words and gripped his rifle hard, staring into the half-dark in search of Hal Coburn whom he had firmly believed to be dead or too badly wounded to have any fight left in him.

Hal recognized the lie. The shot that had felled Bilt had come from behind. It had been a bullet-in-the-back piece of work. Bilt had fallen forwards, without as much as a sound, as if his heart had been ripped out before he knew anything of it.

Hal pondered over the turn in events as he slid further over and then crawled with infinite slowness and in dead silence up the slope in search of a better position. He wanted now to get the last glimmer of the setting sun behind his opponents in the hope that he might catch their movements whilst remaining invisible himself.

It was obvious to him that any sense of loyalty that Pepper might have for his young boss was misplaced. Ross had murdered Bilt for some selfish reason of his own – probably ownership of the gold – and his readiness to lie to Pepper indicated that he might well have a similar fate in store for his second follower.

Was it really the case, though, that Ross believed that he, Hal, was already dead? Perhaps he did and his claim that Hal had shot Bilt was intended merely to divert any suspicion from himself until he had an opportunity to deal with Pepper.

Whatever the situation, Hal had no option but to regard Pepper as an enemy as well as Ross. There was no way in which he could speak to Pepper to tell him what had really happened to Bilt and Pepper had already attempted to kill him and might do so again.

Hal had crawled up the slope and now had a better view of the granite outcrop upon which Ross had stationed himself. It appeared as a grim silhouette against the darkening sky but there was no movement there and no sign now of any glint of metal. He waited in the shadows, eyes peering out into the shortening dusk. Then he heard Pepper's voice raised in a curse far over to his right and the words:

'He ain't here. . . . He's moved, Mr Clement,' and a murmured response that could only have come from Ross.

All right, so they knew he was still alive, and Pepper would remain alive too as long as Ross could make use of him.

There came no further sound for a long time. Twilight gave way to darkness and only the wind in the grasses could be heard. Later came the far-off screech of an owl and then slowly the moon rose above the trees on the horizon, casting an eerie light and long shadows over the landscape. From his position he could make out the dark bulk of an old shack and a length of fencing but nothing else save the scattered stones and coarse vegetation as it caught the faint light.

Now Hal had the moonlight behind him and he lay lower in the shadow of a boulder, fearful that he might be seen. He was determined not to move until he knew where the enemy lay. Long experience in rifle battles throughout such nights had taught him the value of patience. At last he heard pebbles move underfoot and he knew Pepper's anxiety was getting the better of him. Likely enough, Ross Clement, the fast gunfighter, wanted now to bring matters to a head.

As Hal expected it was Pepper who first showed himself. A shadow moved and the moonlight caught the crown of a white hat. Hal waited breathing as softly as a small animal, while the figure rose, half-crouching, and made a stiff, stumbling movement towards the granite slab.

Hal took careful aim. He dared not miss for then he would have two rifles upon him as they picked out his position. He wished with all his heart that Ross was in his gun-sight for there was no doubt that Pepper was being urged forward to set the fight going while his boss remained in hiding, waiting his opportunity.

But there was no time for such niceties. Pepper was out to kill, however foolish his faith in Ross Clement might be . . .

Hal pulled the trigger. Pepper's heart burst

146

violently and poured blood through the back of
his shirt and jacket. He made no sound but a quick
gasping cough and fell amid the stones. His rifle
clattered. Then a bullet smashed into the rock
over Hal's head and he knew the final duel had
begun.

At first, Hal did not move. He knew it was
expected of him and Ross Clement was ready to
shoot again at the first sight of movement. Again
silence fell as each waited for an opportunity.

Clement it was who first lost patience. His
second shot struck almost in the same place as his
first. This time Hal saw the flash and fired instantly
at the point in the shadows from which it had
come, but Clement had ducked and the bullet
ricocheted into the night. Just then a horse
snorted from beyond the old shack and for the
first time Hal knew where the animals had been
tethered.

It struck him that he should get to the horses
before Ross could do so. They offered a possible
means of escape and Hal was determined to deny
his opponent any such opportunity. In a moment,
before Ross raised his head, Hal slid from his
hiding-place and ran doubled up, with one hand
holding his rifle and the other searching for passing support from the boulders, in the direction of
the low building.

He reached it in a headlong scramble just as

another bullet sang overhead. He turned at the corner and lay flat, his rifle again ready for action. He did not consider entering the building. In this light he needed as wide a field of vision as he could get.

Hal guessed Ross's patience was wearing thin and his nerves were becoming ragged. Two bullets thumped into the timbers of the shack as if to prove the point. Again the flash told where Ross lay and Hal returned fire with as much accuracy as the semi-dark allowed. This time there came a sharp yell of pain and a momentary clatter of metal against stone. There was a moment of silence, punctuated only by subdued cursing, before Ross's voice called out, exasperation and pain manifest in its tone.

'Coburn! What the hell is it that you really want out of all this? The gold – or what?'

'To take you in, Clement – that's the full idea! The gold don't mean nothin'. That belongs to the mining company. . . .'

'You still sore about your old man? That had nothin' to do with me – it was Pa – he did all of that!'

'I know it. Your old man has paid for that now, sure enough. This ain't about that any more. Now it's about the Reverend Cranberry and his woman. You murdered them just for your own greed. That's right, ain't it?'

'That goddamned hypocrite and his whore?'

'You murdered them and I'm taking you in for it.'

'What the blazes for? You taking over as sheriff or something?'

'Nope. The law needs to be upheld. That's all.'

'Like Hokay and his bushwhacking?' Ross's voice held a sneer that rang through the night air.

'I guess he paid for that too, although his motives were better than yours.'

There came a further silence, then Ross Clement called out again.

'You a fair man, Coburn? Want to make a stand-up fight of this instead of pot-shotting in the dark? I'll tell you the truth. That last bullet of yours knocked out my left thumb. I cain't use a rifle no more. What about making it with handguns, face to face, gun to gun?'

'What's to stop me shooting you down at this range, Clement?'

'You'll take all night and in the end it will come down to the handguns. You won't ever take me alive, that's for sure.'

Hal knew that much was true. Also, the challenge was difficult to push to one side.

'All right!' he called out. 'You come out first!'

'On the count of three!' came the reply.

They rose together. Hal stood by the corner of the shack, then stepped a little to one side. Ross was in the open, right hand already hovering over his holster, his long shadow cast by the moonlight stretching behind him. He was confident. He expected Hal Coburn to play by the rules and he knew his own mastery with the Colt.

Nevertheless, he was in no mood to pass up any advantage he could gain. He had not been lying about his thumb which pained him badly and he was sick of the whole business, and inwardly blazing with anger over Hal Coburn's interference. . . .

Before another word was said, Ross pulled out his gun and fired, taking Hal completely by surprise. The bullet smashed into Hal's left shoulder and sent him spinning backwards. His own handgun, half-drawn only, fell from its holster to the earth. His legs gave way beneath him and he stumbled into the sawpit, which was looming like a bear-trap behind him.

Hal fell heavily, his already injured shoulder taking the brunt of the fall. He rose up as quickly as he could, recognizing the danger of his position. The agony of his wound ripped through his brain, but he put his hands on the edge of the pit in an attempt to pull himself out of it. The edge was about shoulder-height and presented a major difficulty in his wounded and dazed state but then he dropped his arms as Ross's voice, consumed with laughter, filled the night air.

'Gotcha! I'm standing on your gun, Coburn.

Now I'll finish you for good! Nobody's fault but your own! You should have stayed at home and polished up your medals instead of playing the deputy! Where would you like it – what about straight through the head?'

Hal's mind suddenly drowned in despair. The darkness of the pit in which he crouched seemed all enveloping. He was disarmed. There was nothing to fight with. Instinctively, his hands searched for some weapon, a piece of wood or a stone, anything. His fingers touched cold metal and he grasped an old axe-head which had lain amid the sawdust for years. But what use was it against a Colt, especially one in the hands of Ross Clement?

In a moment would come the bullet and he must plunge into a darkness greater by far than that which surrounded him. . . .

'Mr Hal!' The feeble voice trembled in the night air, like that of some ghost emerging from the grave. Hal looked up over the other edge of the pit and saw some yards away, almost silhouetted against the moon, the figure of horseman, drooping in the saddle, one arm seeming to fall to the ground in weariness, shoulders bent, face in shadow. . . .

'Blick!'

He had no time to say more. Ross Clement's handgun boomed. Blick fell like a stone to the ground.

'Last shot of the war, heh, Coburn!' jeered Clement.

Hal's mind exploded in grief and rage. His hand hurled the iron axe-head. It struck more by luck than good judgement in the centre of Clement's face, breaking his nose and sending blood streaming down his face and neck. Then Hal was out of the sawpit, his anger thrusting all pain aside, and he dived for his gun as it lay on the earth.

His hand grasped it just as Ross Clement recovered from the shock of the axe-head blow. Both guns blazed. Two shots rang out from Clement's weapon, aimed wildly in the direction where Hal had been a moment before but Hal, shooting from ground level, sent a bullet through Ross Clement's lower jaw which smashed its way up through his skull, spattering brains and bone in a bloody arc through the half-dark.

For a moment Hal could not move. He felt stunned with shock and the pain of his shoulder reached a fever pitch but then he forced himself to rise, the faint voice of Blick still in his ears. He turned around and without looking at Clement stumbled towards the inert form of his friend.

Blick lay on his back, the front of his shirt a mass of blood. His eyes were open and stared blindly into the night sky. His lips were parted in that old familiar grin, the whiteness of his teeth still gleaming as the moonlight shone upon his face. Hal fell to his knees, mouth tight, with only a faint groan emanating from his lips while his mind cursed the evil spite of Ross Clement whose last act had been to savagely gun down a wounded and barely conscious man, who had no clear idea of the dangers he had wandered into.

When he got to his feet he stood for a short while, scarcely able to believe that Ross Clement lay dead and all danger was past. He closed Blick's eyes with a terrible feeling of despair. The pony which Blick had ridden and Hal had first seen at Hokay's camp – and later attached to the Reverend Cranberry's buggy – stood silently, glad now to rest from the long trail of that day.

Hal rested too after he had bound up his wounds as best he could. Exhaustion overtook him and he slept until the rising sun came into his eyes. His first act was to lift Blick's body on to the pony. It was not easy for his shoulder ached at every movement, but then it was accomplished and he found his own horse standing amid the stones. He mounted up stiffly and rode silently, leading the pony behind him, back the way he had come the day before.

As he went he could not but think of Blick's journey on that day, when he had struggled through the woods, weighed down by his wound, until he came to the place where Ross Clement had committed his ghastly murders. There he must have found the cowpony and had followed the trail through the long grasses and disturbed stones throughout the long day. In his mind must have been the need to catch up with Hal and to help him if he could. But weakness and exhaustion had taken over his mind so that he had ridden unknowingly into Clement's murderous fire.

The sun was well into the sky when Hal saw the riders approaching. It was the man called Jesset and another whom he did not recognize. Both wore the badges of deputies. They called out to him but he felt too weary to reply until they came to a halt a few yards in front of him. They stared silently for a moment at his bloodstained shirt and exhausted features and then at the still form on the cowpony behind.

'Say, Hal,' said Jesset hesitantly, 'you look bushed. You all right?'

'Well enough to ride,' he replied, moving his lips with difficulty.

'We been following the trail of them horses through the grass . . . the blood too. Somebody bleeding pretty bad?' He broke off and glanced again at Blick. 'He the one or has it been you?'

'Everybody in the end,' replied Hal ruefully. He jerked his head back up the long hillside. 'There are horses way up there at the old shack that need taking in . . . dead guys too. Gold as well, if it's of any interest. '

For a moment they made no reply but gazed into the distance in the direction he had indicated. There were questions in their eyes but they did not voice them in consideration of his weariness.

'Sheriff Somerville is on his way,' said Jesset at last, 'with the rest of the posse. They found the minister and his woman . . . before that, Pete Clement and the little guy called Hokay. What was left, that is! We pushed on a bit to scout out the land. You'll meet the sheriff and the rest of them further down. The girl too. She insisted on coming.' He glanced at Hal's little spark of interest but did not register any thought in his expression. 'Keep on riding slow, Hal, we'll push on to the shack.'

Some time after parting from Jesset and his companion, Hal saw the posse in the distance. There were several horsemen and some spare horses and Hokay's mule. He caught sight of Liza a short distance to the rear of the little cavalcade. Somerville was in the lead and put spurs to his horse when he caught sight of Hal. He arrived a little ahead of the main party.

'Hal, I got to tell you the good news! We found Pete Clement before he died. He told us what really happened that day at Calfskin . . . how the girl was killed and how he deliberately shot your father. Said his conscience had been troubling him for a long time but most of all because his son,

Ross, had shown him what a worthless and point-less life he had led in bringing up a boy who turned out to be such a polecat. Those were his own exact words. He was real bitter!'

Somerville stared at Hal as if expecting a power-ful reaction.

'Old Billy's in the clear,' he pointed out emphat-ically. 'It was all said in front of witnesses. Your father's name is clear at last!'

Hal was looking beyond him at Liza who was making her way past the little column to the front.

'Swell,' he said. 'That's real swell. Better late than never . . .'

Liza was beside him, her eyes full of anxiety. She glanced at the still form of Blick lying over the saddle of the pony, but asked no questions, know-ing this was not the time, although her face showed her grief. Instead, she put out her hand and touched Hal's bloody shirt.

'We need to get you back to Sandstone, Hal,' she said huskily. 'You need that wound dressed prop-erly.'

Hat smiled at her. Their eyes met.

'You'll need a lot of nursing too,' she added.

He put out his hand and held her fingers. They said nothing further until they were well down the trail and out of earshot of the posse riding away from them up the steep slope towards the distant scene of death.

'Feels like I'm just coming home for the first time, Liz.' He smiled. 'Is that what's it's going to be – home at last?'

'It has that kind of a feeling,' she answered, smiling with a quiet understanding.